MR. DARCY AND MR. BINGLEY IN LOVE

MR. DARCY AND MR. BINGLEY IN LOVE

GAY ADVENTURES AT PEMBERLEY

GRIFF HOLLAND

Paperback ISBN: 9798863207605

Cover Design by Etienne St. Aubert

Book Design by Luca Holland

❀ Created with Vellum

TWO-HANDED PLEASURE

As the sun crept through the heavy curtains of his opulent bedroom, casting golden beams across the sheets, Fitzwilliam Darcy awoke in his luxurious bed at Pemberley. He stretched lazily, feeling each sinew ripple beneath his olive skin. His dark locks lay tousled on the pillow, framing his chiseled features and adding to the mystery surrounding this enigmatic gentleman. As his piercing eyes fluttered open, they were met by the sight of his own virile body, muscular and strong.

With a deep inhale, Darcy pulled down the bedsheets, revealing his fully erect 12-inch cock that throbbed with anticipation every morning in the same way. He could never deny himself the opportunity to experience pleasure at this time of morning; it was a ritual he performed without fail. Gripping his manhood firmly with two hands, Darcy began to stroke himself, each motion sending waves of pleasure coursing through his veins.

As he did so, his mind wandered to fantasies of passionate

encounters with other men—feeling their strong arms around him, their warm lips against his, and the ecstasy of surrendering to their desires. He admired men who could only care for their needs with one hand. However, the sizable length and girth of his member necessitated the use of both his muscular arms in the act of pleasure.

"Ah, yes," he whispered, his voice barely audible in the stillness of the morning. His grip tightened as he neared the edge of climax. Finally, he could no longer hold back his release. Hot, sticky cum erupted from his throbbing cock, shooting load after load onto his hairy, muscular chest. He shuddered with a deep satisfaction, basking in the warmth of his spent passion.

Yet, as his heart rate steadied and the flush faded from his cheeks, a melancholy cloud settled over him. For all his good fortune and privileged upbringing, Darcy could not escape the burden of societal expectations. The longing for a genuine romantic connection with another man weighed heavily upon his soul. 'Why must I be confined to a life that does not fulfill me? he pondered his thoughts a whirlwind of emotion.

'Is it impossible to find love and happiness with one who ignites the same fire within me that I feel now?' He sighed, tracing his fingertips along the faint outline of a scar on his chest —a remnant of a forbidden dalliance long ago.

"I cannot continue like this," he whispered aloud to nobody in particular, a tear forming in his eye, "living a lie while my heart yearns for something more."

As he lay there, bared physically and emotionally, Darcy vowed to himself to seek a connection that would bring him true happiness. No longer would he be shackled by the expectations of his peers. He would embrace his desires and find a love that would set his soul alight, for he knew that only then could he be free.

~

LATER THAT DAY, the grand ballroom at Pemberley estate, Mr. Darcy's ancestral home in Derbyshire county, was a scene of luxury and festivity. Candelabras cast dancing shadows on the walls adorned with rich tapestries, while the chandeliers above sparkled like constellations in the night sky. The guests, dressed in their finest silks and satins, moved gracefully across the polished marble floors, their laughter intertwining with the lively melodies played by the orchestra.

Darcy's attention was drawn to the men's attire—he was pleased to note that the latest trend in extremely tight breeches left precious little to the imagination, hugging the curves of their thighs and buttocks and revealing the outlines of their manhood for everyone to see. It was a visual feast for those who dared to let their eyes linger, and many a gentleman found himself stealing furtive glances at his fellows.

Darcy stood near the edge of the dance floor, his thoughts still consumed by his earlier introspection. He sipped his wine, watching the dancers with envy and desire how he longed to find someone who could set his heart aflame, someone whose touch would send shivers down his spine and make him forget the constraints of society.

~

"MR. DARCY, I must say that it is quite the pleasure to see you!" a jovial voice exclaimed.

Turning his gaze toward the source, he beheld Mr. Charles Bingley. The man's muscular stature was evident beneath his finely tailored coat, making it difficult for Darcy not to admire his form. His well-formed chest was practically bursting out of his rather tight blouse. Bingley's curly blond hair was pulled back in a loose and haphazard ponytail, lending him an air of careless charm. His warm smile and bright eyes immediately drew Darcy in.

"Ah, Mr. Bingley, is it not?" Darcy replied, extending a hand. "It is always a delight to have you visit us here at Pemberley."

"Thank you, my dear sir," Bingley said, grasping Darcy's hand firmly. As their fingers touched, a jolt of electricity seemed to pass between them, causing both men to catch their breath. They exchanged glances, each sensing the other's heightened interest and each holding onto the other's hand for just a bit too long.

"Shall we find some ladies to dance with?" Bingley inquired, his voice sultry and inviting. Darcy hesitated for only a moment before nodding in agreement. Bingley grabbed Darcy's arm as he led him to the dance floor. It was a rare opportunity to indulge in the thrill of physical contact, even if only within the boundaries of a formal gesture.

AS THEY LOCATED DANCE PARTNERS, the two men moved to be close to each other and danced to the rhythm of the music. Darcy was entranced by the rosy hue that graced Bingley's cheeks and how his eyes sparkled with excitement. Their bodies occasionally brushed against one another, stirring up a torrent of desire within Darcy.

When a set of vigorous quadrille dances was completed, the musicians took a much-deserved break. It was Darcy's turn to lead Mr. Bingley off by the arm, and he grabbed his rather impressive bicep, squeezing it slightly, which brought a smile to Bingley's face.

In the intimate seclusion along the periphery of the Pemberley dancing room, Mr. Bingley and Mr. Darcy stood nearby. The hushed tones of their conversation mingled with the palpable tension that hung thick in the air, their voices but whispers, as if sharing a clandestine secret.

"Your estate is truly magnificent, Mr. Darcy," Bingley murmured, his voice barely audible, a mere breath caressing the space between them. "But I must admit, it pales compared to its master."

Darcy's countenance betrayed a swift shift in emotion, a flush of warmth spreading across his cheeks, his heart echoing with a rapid, almost thunderous beat. Delivering with such gentle sincerity, the compliment stirred something profound within him.

"I am afraid that you flatter me, Mr. Bingley," he responded, his voice with a subtle hint of flirtation, like a hidden melody beneath his words. "I find myself equally captivated by your presence."

LIKE A PLAYFUL SPRITE, a glimmer danced within Bingley's eyes, illuminating the room with mischievous allure. The corners of his lips curled upward, forming a devilish grin hinting at secrets yet unveiled. His gaze, akin to a feather's gentle caress, flickered downward, drawn to the compelling sight of the burgeoning bulge that strained against the confines of Darcy's impeccably tailored breeches.

The fact that Bingley could not take his glance off his all-too-obvious bulge was making the tightness in his trousers increasingly problematic. It became clear that the desires of the two men began to intertwine in a delicate balance. Bingley's voice, dripping with seductive allure and merriment, broke the charged silence.

"It would appear, my dear sir," he uttered, his words laced with a beguiling invitation, "that *I* am not the sole aroused recipient of the enchantment that this encounter has stirred within us."

Darcy's breath hitched at the subtle insinuation, a bolt of desire shooting through his veins. The shiver that coursed down his spine was both thrilling and intoxicating, as if a veil had been lifted, revealing a hidden realm of forbidden pleasure. Unable to resist the magnetic pull between them, his gaze met Bingley's, a heated stare that mirrored the intensity of their shared longing.

THE TWO MUSCULAR men stood side by side against a wall far from the eyes of the accumulated guests, and their fingers slowly intertwined, their touch lingering, reluctant to sever the connection they had forged. The charged energy that enveloped them crackled in the air, leaving both men yearning for more, their souls entwined in a dance of passion that defied societal constraints.

They acknowledged the undeniable truth in their hearts— their encounter had ignited a flame that could not be extinguished. The allure of their desires beckoned them to explore the uncharted territories of pleasure, to delve into the depths of their shared intimacy. For they had become more than mere acquaintances; they had become kindred spirits, bound by a profound and exhilarating connection that defied the conventions of their time.

An unspoken understanding passed between them, an unquenchable desire that had taken root and grown, intertwining their minds and hearts in an intricate dance of passion. The boundaries of societal expectations and conventional norms blurred, eclipsed by the raw and undeniable pull they felt toward one another.

AS THE NIGHT drew to a close, the whirlwind of the ballroom began to dissipate, and the guests dispersed, their laughter and merriment fading into the distance. Among the remnants of the revelry, Darcy stood, his senses still aflame, his heart pounding within his chest like a wild creature seeking liberation.

"Until next time, Mr. Darcy," Bingley murmured, pressing a chaste kiss to the back of Darcy's hand before disappearing into the crowd.

Bingley's departure had been swift, leaving a lingering imprint of his presence behind. With a murmur that carried the weight of unspoken promises, he pressed his lips gently against the back of Darcy's hand, a chaste caress that sent tremors of anticipation coursing through Darcy's veins. Delicate yet charged with unspoken desire, the touch left an indelible mark upon his being.

A whirlwind of emotions swept through Darcy's mind, his thoughts racing as he watched Bingley disappear into the crowd. What had transpired between them had ignited a fire that refused to be extinguished, a conflagration of longing and possibility that consumed his every waking thought.

FROM THAT BRIEF MOMENT, Darcy's world had shifted, altering the very fabric of his existence. Deep within his soul, he knew that his life would never be as it once was. The magnetic pull he felt towards the dashing Mr. Bingley had forged a connection that transcended societal norms and expectations. It was a bond that whispered of forbidden pleasures and hidden desires, beckoning him to explore uncharted territories of love and intimacy.

As he stood alone amidst the revelry's remnants, the night's echoes still reverberating in his ears, Darcy was consumed by both trepidation and exhilaration. The path before him was uncertain, fraught with challenges and obstacles, but the flame that had been kindled within him burned with an unyielding determination. It was a flame that would guide him into the uncharted depths of his desires, forever altering the course of his life and bringing him closer to the intoxicating allure of Mr. Bingley.

With unwavering determination and a heart set ablaze, Darcy took a deep breath, ready to embark upon a journey that would lead him to the precipice of passion and self-discovery. The night had ended, but the dawn of a new chapter beckoned, promising a love that defied the constraints of their time and a future that held the potential for boundless ecstasy and soulful connection.

Darcy was left amidst the revelry, his heart pounding and his mind racing about what might transpire between him and the dashing Mr. Bingley. The fire ignited within him refused to be extinguished, and he knew that his life would never be the same.

DANCE INTO MY HEART, MR. BINGLEY

The grand ball at Hartford House swirled with vivacious energy, the lively strains of music reverberating through the opulent hall. His refined figure gliding with effortless grace, Darcy was entangled in the whirlwind of each dance. Though his steps led him to various partners throughout the evening, his eyes, like magnetic forces, never strayed far from the captivating presence of Mr. Bingley.

With great trepidation and a glimmer of anticipation, Mr. Darcy acquiesced to the invitation to the grand ball, his heart firmly set on one purpose alone—the prospect of encountering Mr. Charles Bingley amidst the crowd of guests. The event's allure held little appeal for him, for he was a man who found solace in solitude and was unaccustomed to the frivolities of idle chatter and superficial social interactions.

To Darcy, the prospect of attending such affairs often evoked a sense of weariness, a weariness born from a deep-rooted disdain for the insincerity that often prevailed within those glittering halls. The air was thick with pretense, and the dance of casual conversation was a foreign language to his reserved nature. He found himself ill at ease, lacking the easy charm and glib banter that seemed to flow effortlessly from the tongues of those around him.

Yet, within the depths of his soul, a flame of longing burned that compelled him to step into the realm of society. It was a flame fueled by the hope of catching a glimpse of Mr. Charles Bingley, a man whose presence had ignited a fire within him unlike any other. And so, he armed himself with a facade of polite indifference, masking the fervent anticipation that pulsed beneath the surface.

As the night approached, Darcy's apprehension mingled with a growing excitement. His attire, meticulously chosen for the occasion, spoke of his refined taste and understated elegance. Every detail, from the cut of his coat to the pristine whiteness of his cravat, had been meticulously attended to, a testament to his meticulous nature.

Arriving at the ball, Darcy found himself swept into the grandeur of the occasion. The hall was aglow with flickering candles, cascading silk gowns, and the lilting strains of music wading through the air. Couples moved in harmony, their steps guided by a quadrille or a waltz rhythm, while laughter and polite conversation filled the spaces between.

But for Darcy, the grandeur of the ball held little allure. His eyes, ever watchful, scanned the room in search of a familiar figure. It was not the dance that enticed him but the mere possibility of catching sight of Bingley's captivating presence. He longed to see the light in those smoldering eyes, to witness the mischievous curve of those lips that had haunted his dreams.

Amidst the revelry, Darcy felt a palpable tension. He was a

reluctant participant in this charade of social niceties, yearning for a connection that transcended the superficiality of the ballroom. His heart beat with the hope of a profound encounter that would bridge the chasm between their souls and set ablaze the passions that lay dormant within.

AND SO, with a mask of indifference carefully in place, Mr. Darcy ventured forth into the ball, his every step guided by the unspoken desire to find solace in the presence of the man who had sparked a flame within his guarded heart.

As Darcy guided his current dance partner across the polished expanse of the ballroom floor, his gaze remained steadfast, locked onto the smoldering depths of Bingley's eyes. The handsome and muscular blond gentleman, a vision of unbridled vitality, moved with an enthusiasm that stirred something deep within Darcy's core.

Every sinew of Bingley's muscular form was accentuated by the impeccable tailoring of his coat, revealing the strength of his muscles straining to be released from the refined exterior. His golden curls artfully gathered into a carefree ponytail, seemed to dance with him, a radiant halo framing his handsome countenance.

SENSING the intensity of his captivation, Darcy's dancing partner leaned in conspiratorially, her voice calm. "Your friend Mr. Bingley is quite the dancer," she whispered, her eyes following the direction of Darcy's gaze. "He moves with such vigor and enthusiasm."

A strained smile formed at the corners of Darcy's lips, his composure teetering on the edge of unraveling. The mere mention of Bingley's name and the sight of their shared longing stirred a tempest of desires within him. His mind conjured images of a more intimate setting, where their bodies would move sensually, attuned to a melody that existed solely between them.

"Indeed, he does," Darcy replied, his voice conveying tension as he fought to maintain his outward composure. His mind, however, wandered to uncharted territories, where propriety and societal constraints held no sway. In his imagination, he pictured himself entwined with Bingley, their bodies moving, unencumbered by the ballroom's dictates or society's prying eyes.

The dance continued as a mere backdrop to the clandestine desires that swirled within Darcy's heart. With each step, each stolen glance, the connection between them grew stronger, a palpable current that defied the boundaries of friendship. The world around them faded into insignificance as their shared longing threatened to consume them both.

Darcy yearned for a reality where his desires could be realized, where the music that filled the grand hall would serve as a backdrop to their passionate union. The ball may have forced them into the arms of others, but their hearts beat in unison, a silent promise of a future where their bodies would move as one, their souls forever intertwined in a dance of unreserved ecstasy.

As if sensing Darcy's thoughts, Bingley's eyes flicked across the room to meet his once more, and a mischievous grin danced upon his lips. Darcy felt a jolt of desire course through him, his heart pounding at the intensity of their connection.

Throughout the night, as their paths crossed during dances, accidental brushes of fingertips against biceps or knuckles grazing the curve of a hip sent shivers down their spines. The tension between them grew with every touch, becoming a palpable force threatening to consume them.

"Mr. Darcy," Bingley called out, breathless and flushed from dancing, as he approached Darcy near the end of a set. "Might I steal you away for a moment?"

"By all means, Mr. Bingley," Darcy replied, his voice barely concealing his eagerness. As they excused themselves from their respective partners, the two men slipped through a side door of the ballroom and into the moonlit gardens.

Bingley led Darcy to a secluded alcove surrounded by fragrant roses and ivy-covered walls. The intimacy of the space pressed in around them, heightening the illicit thrill that coursed through their veins.

"PRAY, MR. DARCY," Bingley murmured, his voice dipped in a timbre that sent shivers cascading down Darcy's spine, "do tell me, were you as spellbound by the enchantment of our clandestine encounter last week as I found myself to be?"

Darcy's breath hitched within his chest, his heart pounding like a caged creature yearning for release. His eyes, locked in a magnetic gaze with Bingley's, held a vulnerability that betrayed his innermost desires. It was as if a secret language passed between them, unspoken words echoing with the weight of longing and unfulfilled passion.

At that moment, Bingley was absently playing with a button on the front of Darcy's crisp, white shirt, and the touch was driving him mad. At that moment, he was convinced that everyone in the vicinity was observing the lengthening of his manhood in his trousers.

"Spellbound? Perhaps more so, Mr. Bingley," Darcy admitted, his voice laced with a raw honesty that bespoke the intensity of his emotions, "I found myself even more captivated than words could convey."

WITH EACH PASSING MOMENT, the air grew heavier with anticipation, a charged energy that crackled between them. Bingley, encouraged by the palpable connection, closed the distance between them. His presence enveloped Darcy like a warm embrace, their personal spaces merging in a dance of desire and anticipation.

"Then," Bingley breathed, his voice dripping with a heady mixture of need and longing, "allow me to demonstrate just how deeply you have affected me."

The world around them quickly faded into insignificance. Bingley's eyes, darkened with a smoldering fire, traced the contours of Darcy's face, mapping the territory of his longing. Without uttering another word, he closed the remaining distance, his lips claiming Darcy's in a fervent and passionate kiss.

The gathering of people at Hartford House ceased to exist beyond the intoxicating embrace that enveloped them. Lips moved in orchestrated desire, each touch igniting a flame that surged through their veins. It was a kiss that spoke of unspoken promises and a shared understanding of the depths of their connection.

THEN, Darcy surrendered to the overwhelming ecstasy coursing through him. Their bodies pressed closer, their hearts beating in unison, as they explored the depths of their desires and discovered a profound intimacy that transcended societal expectations.

When they finally broke apart, their labored breaths mingling in the air, Darcy's eyes searched Bingley's face, seeking confirmation of the unspoken words that had passed between them. In the depths of Bingley's gaze, he found affirmation, a silent vow that they would navigate the uncharted waters of their desires together.

Within the hallowed walls of their shared passion, Darcy

knew then that their encounter had only served as a prelude to an exquisite symphony of pleasure and intimacy that awaited them in the secret recesses of their hearts.

THE MOMENT their lips converged in a searing union, the veil of social decorum that had once shielded them from their desires dissolved into thin air. Their bodies, aflame with a fervor that defied reason, melded together in an ardent embrace. Surprised by a tide of sensation, Darcy surrendered himself to the intoxicating dance of their tongues, his moans of pleasure mingling with the heady symphony of their desires.

Lost in the depths of their shared passion, Darcy's hands found refuge on the solid expanse of Bingley's broad shoulders, fingertips digging into the fabric of his coat as if desperate to anchor himself amidst the storm of their longing. Bingley, in turn, reveled in the taste and texture of Darcy's mouth, his nimble fingers teasing at the sensitive nape of his neck, eliciting shivers that coursed through his entire being.

"Charles," Darcy breathed, his voice a breathless whisper that carried the weight of unspoken yearning, "you bewitch me with your touch." He had never before experienced a connection so electrifying, so illicit, and it only served to fan the flames of his desire higher, threatening to consume them both.

Reluctantly, Bingley pulled away, their lips parting with a sigh of regret. His chest heaved with the effort to steady his breath, his gaze locked with Darcy's, filled with a potent mixture of longing and the somber recognition of their reality.

"Fitzwilliam," he whispered, the name rolling off his tongue like a benediction, "we must return to the ball before we are missed."

DARCY'S HEART ached at the necessity of their separation, a bittersweet reminder that their stolen moment existed within the confines of secrecy. Though every fiber of his being rebelled against the notion, he understood the weight of societal expectations that bound them. He nodded in reluctant agreement, his eyes flickering with longing and resolve. "Indeed, we must," he conceded, his voice tinged with a sad undertone that mirrored the turmoil within.

The cool night air caressed their heated skin as they emerged from the hidden alcove, a stark reminder of the world they were forced to reenter. Yet, deep within their hearts, the knowledge of their shared passion burned bright, an unquenchable flame that beckoned them to explore the forbidden depths of their desires.

With its polished floors and resplendent chandeliers, the ballroom awaited their return. But a tantalizing promise lingered beyond those walls, in the vast expanse of the world outside, offering a glimpse of what could be if they dared to defy convention and pursue their forbidden love.

They shared a silent agreement between them in the glances, a vow to navigate the treacherous waters of their desires together. And as they stepped back into the grandeur of the ball, their hearts beat in unison, resolute in their determination to seize the passion that awaited them beyond the alcove's shadows.

PLEASURE IN THE CARRIAGE

The carriage plied the uneven road, its rhythmic swaying failing to lull Charles Bingley's restless spirit. His mind, trapped in a tempestuous storm of thoughts, was consumed by the memory of that furtive kiss shared with Mr. Darcy. Like a lingering fragrance, its essence clung to Bingley's lips—a potent blend of temptation and longing that left him aware of his burgeoning desires.

"Damn it all," he muttered, his voice a low murmur that found solace in the confines of the carriage. His fingers clutched the plush upholstery with a frustrated grip as if seeking an anchor amidst the turbulent sea of his emotions. The knowledge of the impropriety that colored his feelings weighed heavily upon him, yet he could not ignore the magnetic force that inexorably drew him closer to Fitzwilliam Darcy.

As the verdant countryside passed by in a blur beyond the carriage windows, Bingley's mind replayed the stolen moments shared in secret. He recalled the electric charge that coursed through his veins as their lips converged, the dance of their tongues a testament to their shared desires. Each stolen touch, each whispered word, had served as kindling to the fire that roared within him, consuming his reason and awakening a hunger he had never known.

But society, with its rigid expectations and narrow-minded judgments, cast a shadow upon their connection. Bingley understood the weight of their predicament, the precariousness of their position as men of privilege. It was a world that demanded conformity, that stifled the flame of love and passion that dared burn outside the boundaries of convention.

Yet, despite the societal strictures that threatened to extinguish their desires, Bingley found himself unable to deny the pull of his heart. The more he tried to resist, the stronger the gravitational force that drew him to Darcy became. It was as if the universe itself conspired to bring them together, tempting them with a love that defied the constraints of their time.

WITH EACH PASSING MILE, the disquiet in Bingley's soul intensified. His thoughts, a chaotic whirlwind, tugged at the edges of his consciousness, urging him to acknowledge the depths of his feelings. Like a cocoon of contemplation, the carriage shielded him from the prying eyes of the world outside, affording him a brief respite to confront his truth.

And as the carriage rolled on, carrying him closer to the inevitability of their reunion, Bingley knew that the path before him was uncertain. It was a journey that would challenge not only the confines of society but also the depths of his courage. But he could no longer deny the allure of Darcy's presence, the magnetic pull that beckoned him to explore the uncharted territories of their forbidden desires.

The road stretched ahead, winding and uncertain, mirroring

the path before them. Bingley's heart beat with both trepidation and hope, for he knew that their passion was not a fleeting fancy but a flame that burned with an intensity that promised to illuminate their lives.

And so, as the carriage pressed forward, Bingley resolved to face the tempest that awaited him. For standing on the precipice of a love that defied the conventions of their time, he understood that the true measure of a man was not in his ability to conform but in his willingness to embrace his truth, even if it meant defying the expectations of a world that sought to smother the flames of desire.

AS THE EBONY shroud of night descended upon the elegant carriage, Bingley, his senses aflame with desire, succumbed to an irrepressible surge of lust that coursed through his very veins. Ensuring his privacy with a final, lingering glance at the closed curtains, he dared to surrender to the intoxicating pull of his yearning. The buttons of his trousers were carefully undone, allowing his engorged manhood to spring forth, the sight and touch of it serving only to amplify the intensity of his arousal.

"God, Fitzwilliam," he whispered with fervor, his voice a breathless invocation, as his hand began its enchanting dance upon his throbbing length. The clandestine nature of their illicit connection served as kindling for his imagination, conjuring vivid images of Darcy's commanding presence, his firm and skillful hands traversing Bingley's form with an ardent possessiveness that stirred his very core.

Within the peaceful confines of the carriage, Bingley's impassioned moans and breathy reveries filled the air, an intoxicating symphony punctuated by the gentle sounds of flesh upon flesh as he deftly pleasured himself. The vision of Darcy's sinewy physique pressed against his own, their bodies melded in an embrace of unbridled ardor, their lips fused in a tempest of insatiable passion, ignited an undeniable urgency in his actions.

With each stroke of his hand, Bingley's mind became a canvas upon which desire painted its most tantalizing scenes. He envisioned the taut contours of Darcy's musculature, his grip's firmness, and their entwined bodies' unyielding heat. The symphony of their shared pleasure crescendoed in his mind, reaching a fevered pitch that mirrored the crescendo building within his being.

OH, how he longed to taste the forbidden fruits of their union, to succumb to the rapturous bliss that awaited him. In the dimly lit carriage, his body became a temple of sensuality, his hand a willing acolyte guiding him toward the precipice of ecstasy. With each stroke, each whispered plea, Bingley surrendered himself to the whirlwind of his desires, his body and soul consumed by an all-encompassing yearning for the touch and embrace of his beloved Fitzwilliam Darcy.

"Ah, Fitzwilliam..." Bingley gasped, his strokes becoming more erratic, his breathing more ragged. As the fantasy peaked, he imagined Darcy taking him, their bodies united in sinful ecstasy, with whispered declarations of love falling from their lips. The mere thought was enough to send Bingley over the edge, his seed spilling onto the carriage floor in a charged ejaculation.

Panting heavily, he stared at the mess he had made with a mixture of embarrassment and satisfaction. He knew that the path he now found himself on was fraught with danger and societal disapproval, but the yearning in his heart could not be contained any longer.

"Damn propriety," he whispered fiercely as he buttoned up his trousers and tried to regain some semblance of composure.

"Fitzwilliam Darcy has awakened something within me, and I will not rest until I know the full extent of this passion."

As the carriage continued its journey through the night, Charles Bingley sat in quiet contemplation, his heart filled with anticipation and longing. One thing was sure: the road ahead would be uncertain, but the allure of Fitzwilliam Darcy made every risk seem worth taking.

"God help us both," he murmured, staring out into the darkness, eager for the sun to rise and illuminate the next chapter of their passionate love affair.

"AH, MR. DARCY!" Charles Bingley exclaimed as he gracefully entered the opulent drawing room at Pemberley the following morning, his eyes immediately riveted to the tall and commanding figure of Fitzwilliam Darcy. His heart quickened at the sight, for within the recesses of his being, he concealed a secret desire that burned with an intensity known only to him.

"Good morning, Mr. Bingley," replied Darcy, a subtle yet captivating smile adorning his lips. The morning light cast a radiant glow upon his countenance, rendering him all the more alluring. "I trust you found repose during the night, kind sir?"

"Indeed, I did, sir," Bingley confessed, a faint chuckle escaping his throat. Yet, concealed behind his mirthful facade, a rosy hue suffused his cheeks, an undeniable testament to the memories that lingered from the previous night. His gaze, like a magnet drawn to its counterpart, descended upon the fit of Darcy's trousers, which, in their valiant struggle, barely contained the generous bulge that lay beneath.

Bingley's senses were awash with recollections of their shared dance, the memory of Darcy's manhood asserting its presence with a potency that commanded his attention, akin to a steadfast lighthouse guiding him through the tumultuous sea of his most fervent desires.

THOUGH THE WORLD around them remained blissfully unaware of the captivating play of emotions in Bingley's heart, he could not suppress the churning storm within him. Each stolen glance, each brush of their bodies, resonated deep within his soul, whispering of unspoken longings and uncharted territories yearning to be explored.

Bingley's fingers itched to trace the contours of Darcy's form; his lips ached to taste the sweetness of their forbidden union. And yet, the world they inhabited demanded their masks of civility, disguising the passion that smoldered beneath the surface.

As the two handsome men exchanged pleasantries, their dialogue danced upon the air, concealing the tempestuous undercurrent that surged between them. Each word, each subtle gesture, was laden with meaning, carrying the weight of their unspoken desires. For within the depths of their souls, Bingley and Darcy were bound by a connection that transcended societal norms, a connection where their bodies yearned to entwine; their hearts longed to beat as one.

"IS SOMETHING AMISS?" Darcy inquired, his dark eyes shimmering with intrigue and concern as they met Bingley's lingering gaze. Like a delicate tangle of silk threads, the intensity of their connection hung in the air, poised to unravel a secret that lay heavy upon Bingley's heart.

"Not at all, sir," Bingley replied with haste, realizing he had been caught admiring the snug fit of Darcy's breeches. He forced himself to gaze away, attempting to compose himself. "It is but the fervor that accompanies each day in your delightful company, I assure you."

A knowing smile played upon Darcy's lips, a silent acknowledgment passing between them. "Ah, yes," he murmured, his voice laced with a tantalizing hint of mischief. "And perchance, the clandestine nature of our connection adds a certain ... zest to our every encounter, would you not concur?"

Bingley's heart quickened at Darcy's words, a thrill coursing through him at the mere mention of their shared secret. The audacity of their actions, the stolen kiss that lingered as an indelible mark upon his memory, ignited a fiery surge of exhilaration within him. To be trapped in such a forbidden web, where societal expectations were cast aside, was a heady elixir intoxicating his very being.

"YES, INDEED, QUITE SO, SIR," Bingley agreed, his voice betraying a tremor of excitement. He dared not reveal the depths of his desire, the consuming longing that had taken root within him. But in Darcy's presence, it was as if the world had been reimagined, their connection a beacon guiding him towards uncharted territories of pleasure.

Darcy's eyes sparkled with an understanding that surpassed the spoken word, an invitation veiled within the honeyed tones of his voice. "Shall we retreat to the sanctuary of the library, where quiet conversation may flourish?" he suggested, his words imbued with a subtle yet undeniable undercurrent of innuendo. The suggestion sent delicious shivers cascading down Bingley's spine, his imagination conjuring a tapestry of possibilities.

"An excellent proposition, Mr. Daryc," Bingley responded eagerly, his heart pulsating with anticipation. To be enveloped in the hallowed walls of the library, where knowledge and desire intertwined, was an invitation he could not refuse. He yearned to surrender himself to the enchantment of Darcy's presence, to indulge in the tête-à-tête that promised to unravel the secret desires that bound them.

And so, they departed from the drawing room, their steps

echoing down the grand corridor, a symphony of anticipation reverberating within their souls. Behind the closed doors of the library, their shared secret would find solace, their connection blossoming in the hushed whispers and stolen glances that painted the canvas of their intimacy.

As they crossed the threshold into the library, Darcy's movements possessed a grace that bespoke his innate elegance. With a deliberate sweep of his hand through the dark locks that framed his countenance, he unveiled the strong curve of his neck, exposing a tantalizing hint of stubble that graced his jawline. The sight beckoned to Bingley, igniting a torrent of desires that swirled within his being. Oh, to run his fingers through those thick tresses, to feel the silken strands entwined with his while claiming Darcy's mouth with his own, delving into the depths of their forbidden passions.

"Mr. Bingley," Darcy began his voice a low and intimate murmur that sent tremors coursing through Bingley's veins. Leaning closer, their proximity becoming an intoxicating dance of desire, he continued, "I must confess, our encounter of last evening has left an indelible mark upon my very being."

"An indelible mark?" Bingley echoed, his pulse quickening at the warmth of Darcy's breath upon his skin, their shared breath mingling in the air.

"Indeed," Darcy whispered, his eyes flickering downward, briefly capturing the glistening curve of Bingley's lips before rising to meet his gaze once more. "It appears that we have unearthed a shared appetite that transcends the bounds of societal expectations, a hunger that yearns to be sated in the realms of impropriety."

THE WEIGHT of Darcy's confession hung heavily in the air, eliciting a myriad of emotions that surged within Bingley's chest. A single tear welled in his eye, a testament to the overwhelming intensity of his affection, and swiftly cascaded down his cheek, a crystalline declaration of his vulnerability. In that poignant moment, Darcy could no longer bear the torment that gripped his own heart. Driven by a fervor that surpassed reason, he reached out, his fingertips delicately capturing the tear as it traced its path upon Bingley's face.

In that tender gesture, an unspoken language flowed between them, a language that transcended societal boundaries and societal norms. Their connection, forged in secrecy and kindled by shared desire, trembled with the promise of an intimacy that defied the conventions of their time. It was a connection that whispered of a love that dared to exist beyond the confines of their world, where their hearts could intertwine without fear of reproach.

The library, a silent witness to their stolen moments, stood as a sanctuary for their desires, its walls echoing with the weight of their unspoken longings. Within its hallowed space, Bingley and Darcy would embark upon a journey of exploration, their bodies and souls converging in a dance of passion that would leave an indelible mark upon their lives.

"AH, MR. DARCY," Bingley sighed, his voice heavy with a mixture of longing and anticipation as his body stirred with desire within the confines of his trousers. The mere thought of indulging in their mutual cravings ignited a fire deep within him that threatened to consume his every thought and action. "You speak of a hunger that resonates within the depths of my being, a hunger that I find increasingly difficult to ignore."

Darcy's eyes gleamed with a predatory glint, a simmering intensity mirrored Bingley's yearning. His voice, a velvet caress that cascaded shivers down Bingley's spine, filled the hallowed space around them. "Perhaps it is time, dear Bingley, that we quench this insatiable thirst that binds us," he murmured, his words hanging in the air like a whispered incantation, their potency electrifying the atmosphere between them.

"Indeed," Bingley agreed, his heartbeat thundering in his ears, each pulse a testament to the anticipation coursing through his veins. The allure of their forbidden desires beckoned to him, promising a journey into uncharted realms of pleasure, where the boundaries of convention and restraint would fade into insignificance. "Let us partake of this forbidden fruit, Mr. Darcy, and savor the heady sweetness that blooms from our secret desires."

With that, a pact unspoken but undeniable was forged between them. The world around them ceased to exist as they surrendered to the intoxicating dance of their shared passion. In the private sanctum of their desires, they embarked upon a journey fraught with the thrill of the unknown, where the constraints of society held no dominion, and their bodies became vessels for unadulterated pleasure.

BINGLEY AND DARCY discovered the depths of their desires, their bodies merging in a symphony of intertwined limbs and fervent whispers. The library, with its shelves laden with knowledge and secrets alike, bore witness to their union, its silent walls echoing their gasps of pleasure and the whispered declarations of their love.

As their bodies entwined and their souls merged, they found solace in each other's arms, their union a refuge from a world that denied their truth. In their shared passion, they reveled in the liberation of their desires, embracing the exhilarating freedom of surrendering to the all-consuming fire that burned between them.

And so, they embarked on a journey that would forever alter the course of their lives. In their shared ecstasy, they discovered the boundless heights of pleasure and the profound connection that transcended physicality. In their love, they found solace, strength, and resolute defiance against a world that sought to confine them.

TAKE ME, MR. DARCY!

As Darcy and Bingley retreated further into the seclusion of a dimly lit alcove, a haven hidden from prying eyes, the distant melodies of the ballroom faded into a mere whisper, drowned by sounds of their desires. The tendrils of shadow that enveloped them seemed to unite their bodies, weaving an ethereal tapestry that merged their very beings. In the clandestine sanctuary they had found, they exchanged heated glances, each glance a silent promise that stirred the depths of their souls.

"Charles," Darcy's voice, low and husky, brushed against the sensitive flesh of Bingley's ear, sending tremors of anticipation coursing through him. "Do you truly wish to embark upon this arduous journey with me? It is a path fraught with peril and secrecy, where society's watchful eyes may seek to condemn us. But it is also a path that holds the promise of unfathomable pleasure, where the depths of our desires can be explored without restraint."

Bingley's breath hitched at the weight of Darcy's words, his heart pounding like a wild beast longing for freedom. He turned his gaze to meet Darcy's, their eyes locked in an intense exchange, a silent understanding transcending spoken language's boundaries. In that moment, the world around them ceased to exist, their connection forged through shared longing and unspoken truths.

"Fitzwilliam," Bingley finally replied, his voice a mere breath, his eyes fixated on Darcy's lips' full, inviting curve. "I can conceive of no greater adventure than the one that beckons us now, that which we stand upon the precipice of. It is a journey that promises the thrill of stolen moments and the ecstasy of uncharted territories. To deny such a path would be to deny the very essence of our beings."

~

WITH THOSE WORDS hanging in the air, pregnant with desire, Bingley closed the remaining distance between them. Their bodies collided, their lips meeting in an ecstatic union that defied the constraints of their world. It was a kiss filled with the fiery passion that had smoldered within them for far too long, a kiss that spoke of longing, surrender, and the unspoken promise of a love that dared to defy societal expectations.

In that embrace, time stood still. The world outside their secluded haven ceased to exist, replaced by a realm of heightened sensations and unbridled pleasure. Their lips moved in a dance of fervor and urgency, their tongues entwined in an exploration of shared secrets and forbidden desires. With each caress and passionate sigh, they unveiled a realm of intimacy that defied the conventions of their time, a domain where their bodies melded in an exquisite symphony of desire.

Within the alcove's embrace, Bingley and Darcy embarked upon a journey of sensual discovery, their bodies entangled in a tapestry of limbs and whispered confessions. It was a journey that would test their mettle, demanding secrecy and resilience. Still, above all, it was a journey that promised undeniable pleasure and the unrivaled ecstasy of a love that refused to be silenced.

And so, their lips remained locked in an embrace that bridged the realms of passion and vulnerability, their union a testament to the power of love and the strength found within the embrace of another. They would find solace and liberation in the depths of their desires, defying societal expectations and forging their path toward a love that would forever illuminate their hearts.

THE TASTE of Darcy's mouth was intoxicating, eliciting an audible moan from Bingley as their tongues tangled in a dance of lustful exploration. Darcy's strong hands found their way to Bingley's waist, gripping and pulling him closer until there remained no distance between their bodies. The hardness pressing against Bingley's thigh left no doubt as to the effect their embrace had on the enigmatic Mr. Darcy.

"Allow me, dear Bingley, to reveal the depths of my desire," Darcy murmured, his breath mingling with the warmth of Bingley's lips as he tenderly pressed against them. His hand ventured beneath the waistband of Bingley's trousers, his fingers tracing a tantalizing path along the delicate expanse of skin just below Bingley's navel. It was a touch that kindled flames of longing, igniting a fire that threatened to consume them both.

Barely able to contain his response, Bingley gasped, his senses ablaze as Darcy's skilled fingers continued their torturous descent. They traveled with purpose, guided by an intimate knowledge of Bingley's most secret desires, until they found their destination, wrapping around Bingley's throbbing erection. A surge of pleasure coursed through him, an electric current that left him reeling with need.

"It appears, my dear Bingley, that our tryst has taken its toll on you as well," Darcy observed, a mischievous smile dancing upon his lips as he maintained his gentle grip, his fingers caressing Bingley's length with a maddening slowness. The intoxicating rhythm of his stroking was a symphony of exquisite torment, each deliberate movement designed to elicit the most vibrant of responses. "Tell me, Charles, what is it that you want? What do you crave in this moment of unreserved intimacy?"

BINGLEY'S VOICE strained with a potent cocktail of desire and longing, trembled as he surrendered to the consuming sensations that washed over him. "Your touch, sir," he admitted, a raw honesty infusing his words. "I want to feel your hands upon me, claiming every inch of my being. I want your touch to ignite a fire that burns my soul."

A wicked glimmer danced in Darcy's eyes, his lips curving into a knowing smile. He understood the depth of Bingley's yearning, for it mirrored his own, and he would grant those desires without hesitation. With a deliberate increase in the intensity of his strokes, he seized Bingley's passion in his hand, a masterful conductor commanding a symphony of pleasure.

"Your wish is my command," Darcy replied, his voice laced with a heady mixture of authority and adoration. The teasing intensity of his touch grew, each stroke a testament to his unwavering dedication to Bingley's pleasure. The rhythm of their shared ardor quickened, their bodies moving in a harmony that defied the world's constraints beyond their hidden sanctuary.

In that timeless moment, the boundaries of decency dissolved, replaced by the undeniable truth of their connection. Bingley surrendered to the intoxicating sensations that enveloped him, his body a canvas upon which Darcy painted a masterpiece of desire. With each stroke, each caress, the intensity of their passion surged, drawing them closer to a precipice where ecstasy awaited.

And so, amidst the hushed whispers of their shared ecstasy,

the boundaries of their desires blurred, and they surrendered to a world where pleasure reigned supreme. In the tender strokes and impassioned gasps, they found solace, fulfillment, and a love that defied the conventions of their time.

As BINGLEY SOUGHT support against the wall, his senses aflame with desire, Darcy's free hand embarked on a daring exploration beneath the fabric of Bingley's shirt. His fingers, nimble and purposeful, navigated the landscape of Bingley's chest until they found their target—a sensitive nipple ripe for his touch. With an artful blend of pressure and precision, Darcy's thumb and forefinger pinched and rolled the nub, coaxing forth moans of pleasure from Bingley's lips. The sensations reverberated through Bingley's body, electrifying every nerve and igniting a fire that threatened to consume him whole. He instinctively bucked into Darcy's firm grip in response, his body aching for more.

"Fitzwilliam... I... I cannot bear this exquisite torture any longer," Bingley gasped, his voice a desperate plea, his mind clouded with an overwhelming surge of desire. He yearned for release, for the culmination of their shared passion, and the tantalizing caress of Darcy's fingers upon his nipple had pushed him perilously close to the edge. "I need... I need more, Fitzwilliam. I need you."

A mischievous glint danced in Darcy's eyes as he reveled in his power over Bingley, the power to unravel him with a simple touch, to awaken the depths of his longing. He seared a searing kiss upon the tender expanse of Bingley's neck, a testament to his dominance and a promise of what was to come. But instead of yielding to Bingley's urgent pleas, Darcy sank to his knees, his movements deliberate and tantalizingly slow.

"Patience, my love," Darcy teased, his voice a seductive murmur that sent shivers cascading down Bingley's spine.

"Patience, I am here to provide you the satisfaction you so desperately crave."

~

As DARCY POSITIONED himself before Bingley, their eyes locked in an embrace of shared desires, Bingley's breath hitched in anticipation. He marveled at the sight before him—the enigmatic and powerful Fitzwilliam Darcy, poised on the precipice of fulfilling their most illicit fantasies. With an agility born of experience, Darcy skillfully released Bingley's pulsing manhood from its confining garments, exposing the length of their shared passion to the air.

It was a sight that stirred Bingley's core, rendering him breathless with a heady mixture of desire and vulnerability. Before him stood a man of undeniable allure, who commanded respect and adoration and offered himself willingly to fulfill Bingley's most intimate cravings. The moment's weight settled upon them, a palpable tension that hung in the air as Bingley surrendered himself to the unknown, to the pleasures that awaited him.

In that hushed moment, as Darcy prepared to take Bingley into his mouth, their connection transcended the boundaries of their bodies. It was a communion of souls, an unspoken promise of trust and surrender. Bingley's heart raced with trepidation and anticipation; his senses heightened as he prepared to experience pleasure unlike any he had known.

~

"ARE YOU PREPARED, CHARLES?" Darcy inquired, his warm breath caressing Bingley's exposed length, a tantalizing promise of the pleasure to come.

Bingley's voice, barely above a whisper, trembled with a mixture of desire and anticipation. "More than you can imagine," he confessed, his heart racing in his chest, every fiber craving the release that awaited him.

No sooner had the words escaped Bingley's lips than Darcy's mouth, warm and wet, descended upon him, engulfing him in a sea of sensation. Waves of pleasure coursed through Bingley's body, each flick of Darcy's skilled tongue and every suction of his lips an exquisite torment that threatened to consume him entirely. The world around them melted away, leaving only the primal connection between two souls bound by love and desire.

With a graceful descent, Darcy's lips parted, welcoming Bingley's throbbing manhood into their warmth and wetness. The sensation was an intoxicating blend of heat and pressure, an exquisite dance of pleasure that eclipsed their most vivid imaginings. As Darcy's skilled mouth enveloped him, Bingley was lost in a world where all that mattered was the symphony of sensations that consumed him. It was a world where boundaries were shattered, where societal constraints evaporated, leaving only two souls entwined in a dance of raw desire and unadulterated passion.

As Darcy navigated the landscape of Bingley's arousal with an expertise born of experience, Bingley's certainty solidified— there could be no going back to a life devoid of these stolen moments of passion. The depth of their connection and the profound intimacy they shared forever changed him. In the sanctuary of their forbidden desires, Bingley found solace, fulfillment, and love that eclipsed the boundaries of their time.

"FITZWILLIAM," Bingley moaned with need and longing, his fingers entangled in Darcy's dark curls as he surrendered to the intoxicating pleasure. "I... I am on the edge."

Darcy's gaze, unwavering and filled with a tenderness that spoke volumes, locked with Bingley's. He continued his relentless ministrations, his mouth a conduit of pleasure, his eyes a steady anchor in the tumultuous sea of sensation. He understood the delicate balance between fun and surrender, the significance of this pivotal moment in their shared ecstasy.

"Then let go, Charles," Darcy urged his lover, his voice a gentle command that ignited the embers of Bingley's passion. "Surrender yourself to the rapture that awaits you. Allow me the privilege of tasting your pleasure, of witnessing your complete abandon."

As their eyes remained locked in an unbreakable gaze, Bingley succumbed to the overwhelming surge of pleasure that consumed him. He released the reins of control, allowing the currents of ecstasy to carry him away. His body trembled with the intensity of his climax, every nerve alight with a symphony of sensations. And as his essence spilled forth, Darcy drank from the source of Bingley's pleasure, a communion that transcended the physical act—a union of souls bound by a love that defied the constraints of their world.

With a final cry of ecstasy, Bingley had surrendered to the waves of pleasure that coursed through him, spilling his release into Darcy's eager mouth. As Darcy swallowed every last drop, their bond grew stronger, their connection forged in the fires of their secret love.

"Thank you, Fitzwilliam," Bingley panted, his breaths still ragged from the explosive climax.

"Anything for you, Charles," Darcy replied, rising to his feet and drawing Bingley into a tender embrace. "Our journey has only just begun."

In their shared vulnerability and raw intimacy, Bingley understood the power of their connection. The connection thrived in the shadows, where their deepest desires found solace and fulfillment. They had dared to defy society's expectations, to embrace a love that surpassed the boundaries imposed upon them. And in the culmination of their shared passion, they discovered a freedom transcending the limitations of a world that sought to keep them apart.

DARE TO DREAM, CHARLES

As the sun gracefully descended upon the verdant landscape of Pemberley, casting a warm glow through the tall windows, Darcy and Bingley sought refuge in the seclusion of Darcy's resplendent study. The room exuded an air of refinement, its shelves lined with leather-bound tomes that whispered tales of knowledge and secrets. Various scents filled the air—a heady blend of aged parchment, polished wood, and the lingering aroma of fine claret. Within this sanctuary of intellect and intimacy, the two gentlemen found solace, their conversation a delightful interplay of sharp minds and quick wit.

Seated in plush armchairs, their forms bathed in the soft flicker of firelight, Darcy and Bingley indulged in the pleasures of both discourse and libation. Their glasses, filled with the ruby elixir of claret, were raised in a toast to the camaraderie they shared, to the bonds forged in the crucible of forbidden desires.

"Fitzwilliam," Bingley began his voice a melodic caress that hung in the air, his gaze fixed upon Darcy with an unquenchable curiosity. "I find myself irresistibly drawn to inquire ... when did you first become aware that your desires, as you so eloquently put it, were different from societal expectations?"

Darcy, a man of measured reserve, paused for a fleeting moment, his eyes cast downward as he considered his response. The weight of truth settled upon his broad shoulders, the memories of a long past resurfacing with poignant clarity. He answered with a breath as steady as the ticking of a pocket watch; his voice tinged with vulnerability and honesty.

"IT WAS during my formative years at Eton," Darcy confessed, his voice a low murmur that carried the weight of a secret shared. "In the hallowed halls of that esteemed institution, I was assigned to share a room with a young man of incomparable beauty, a creature who defied the conventions of mere mortals. As the moon ascended and the world slumbered, we stole clandestine moments—moments suffused with passion and unspoken longing. In the stillness of those stolen nights, we dared to explore the depths of our desires, unburdened by the weight of societal expectations."

Bingley listened, rapt and captivated, to Darcy's confession. His heart quickened with empathy and desire, an understanding that transcended words. He had traversed the corridors of yearning, discovering his truth amidst the shadows of a world that demanded conformity.

Their shared revelations forged a bond, a fragile thread of understanding and acceptance that wove them together. In that study, steeped in intellectual pursuits and adorned with the traces of their shared passions, they found solace in each other's presence. They were kindred spirits, two souls unafraid to venture beyond the boundaries of what was deemed proper, two hearts that beat in unison, craving the forbidden.

And so, as the sun dipped below the horizon, casting a

tapestry of twilight hues across the land, Darcy and Bingley continued their tête-à-tête, savoring the richness of their connection. In the depths of their shared desires, in the sanctuary of their stolen moments, they discovered a love that defied the strictures of their time. This love whispered of liberation, of the transformative power of surrender.

"AH, MY DEAR CHARLES," Bingley mused, his voice infused with a sense of wonder, his gaze lingering upon the depths of his wineglass. "How remarkable that our paths have converged, that we now partake in these stolen moments of passion."

Darcy, his countenance alight with a flame of ardor, nodded in agreement, his eyes fixed upon Bingley with an intensity that bespoke his longing. "Indeed," he acknowledged his voice a low timbre laced with desire. "But, my dearest Charles, I yearn for more than mere stolen moments with you. I crave a life where our love can flourish openly, where we may share our joys and sorrows without the shadows of secrecy."

Bingley's heart quickened at Darcy's words, the fervent declaration of a desire that echoed his deepest yearnings. He set his wineglass aside, its ruby contents momentarily forgotten, and met Darcy's gaze with unwavering determination. "Is such a life within our grasp, sir?" he whispered the words a fragile hope that hung in the air. "Can we dream of a future where our love finds its rightful place, even in a world that seeks to deny it?"

Darcy's visage took on a pensive cast, his brows furrowing as he considered the complexities of their predicament. The weight of society's disapproval, the whispered judgments that lurked within the corridors of privilege, threatened to cast a pall over their aspirations. Yet, he refused to surrender hope.

"PERHAPS, CHARLES," Darcy mused, his voice laced with a tempered optimism. "True, the world may not readily embrace our love, but that does not mean we cannot carve out our path to happiness. We must be circumspect, of course, and exercise caution in our endeavors. But, my dear Charles, do not doubt the power of our love to overcome the obstacles before us."

Bingley's gaze, a mix of trepidation and unwavering devotion, met Darcy's with an unwavering resolve. "Then let us be brave, Fitzwilliam," he implored, his voice filled with a quiet determination that matched his lover's. "Let us face the challenges that lie ahead, side by side, our hearts entwined in a love that refuses to be silenced."

Darcy's hand, warm and strong, reached out to clasp Bingley's, their fingers intertwining in a tangible bond that mirrored the intangible connection of their souls. "Agreed," he replied, his voice resolute. "We shall tread this path together, fortified by our love, with a steadfastness that defies the expectations of a world that would keep us apart. As partners in love and life, we shall navigate the intricate dance of society, our hearts unyielding in their pursuit of happiness."

"CHARLES," Darcy whispered, his voice thick with emotion, "I have never felt more alive than when I am with you. You have awakened something deep within me, something I feared would remain hidden forever."

"William," Bingley replied, his voice trembling with emotion, "I feel the same. With you, I have discovered a part of myself that I never knew existed, and I cherish every moment we share."

In that instant, their lips met, and the passion that had simmered beneath the surface erupted in a torrent of desire. As they kissed, their hands roamed over each other's bodies, seeking out every curve, every contour, every exquisite inch of flesh. And yet, even as they surrendered to the carnal pleasures of the flesh, there was an undercurrent of deeper emotion that infused every touch, every caress, every shared breath.

"Tonight, Charles," Darcy murmured between kisses, "let us forge our bond anew, not just as lovers, but as soulmates."

"Let it be so, Fitzwilliam," Bingley agreed, his heart pounding wildly as the longing between them swept him away.

And as the night deepened, Darcy and Bingley embarked on a journey of discovery, passion, and unbreakable love, determined to face whatever challenges lay ahead, together and undaunted.

THE NIGHT HAD DEEPENED, its ebony folds caressing the estate of Pemberley with a sensual touch as if the air were charged with anticipation. Within the confines of his bedchamber, Fitzwilliam Darcy paced like a caged animal, the smoldering fire in his heart fanned to a blazing inferno by memories of stolen kisses and whispered promises. The passion between him and Charles Bingley was undeniable, but the constraints of society threatened to suffocate it like a corset pulled too tight.

"Damn this world and its expectations," Darcy muttered under his breath, his chest heaving with frustration. "What I would give for the freedom to love without fear or shame."

"Fitzwilliam?" came a hesitant voice from the doorway, followed by the soft rustle of fabric as Bingley stepped into the room, closing the door behind him. His face was flushed, and his eyes were alight with excitement and trepidation.

"Charles, what are you doing here?" Darcy asked in hushed tones, his heart pounding at the sight of the man who had captured his soul.

"Can we not simply be together?" Bingley pleaded, his muscular arms encircling Darcy's waist, drawing them close. "I cannot bear another moment apart from you."

"Nor I," Darcy admitted, his breath hitching as their bodies pressed against one another. The heat between them was palpable, a living, breathing entity that demanded satisfaction. And yet, Darcy knew all too well the danger they faced should their secret be discovered.

~

"LISTEN, MY LOVE," he said, his voice low and urgent. "We must tread carefully, lest our happiness be snatched away by the cruel hand of fate. The world is not yet ready for a love such as ours."

"Then let us make our world, Fitzwilliam," Bingley murmured, his lips brushing against Darcy's earlobe, sending shivers down his spine. "One where we are free to love and be loved in return."

As their mouths met in a searing kiss that threatened to consume them both, Darcy's mind raced with the enormity of what they were proposing. Could they genuinely defy society and forge a new path for themselves? Or would they be forever doomed to hide their love in shadows and stolen moments?

"Charles," Darcy whispered, his hands trembling as they caressed the broad expanse of Bingley's chest. "I do not know if it is possible, but I swear this: I will fight to my dying breath for our right to love one another."

"Promise me, Fitzwilliam," Bingley said, his voice choked with emotion. "Promise me that no matter what obstacles we face, we will never let go of each other."

"I promise," Darcy vowed, sealing his words with a fierce and possessive kiss that left them both gasping for air.

~

AND THEN, without warning, a loud knock at the door shattered their fragile world, pulling them back to reality like a cold splash of water.

"Mr. Darcy!" called Caroline Bingley's voice from the hallway. "May I have a moment of your time?"

Darcy's heart clenched in terror, the implications of her presence all too clear. Had she discovered their secret? Would she expose them to the world?

"Fitzwilliam," Bingley murmured, his eyes wide with fear as he stepped back from their embrace, hastily adjusting his disheveled clothes.

"Go," Darcy urged him, his voice shaking. "Hide in the dressing room. I will deal with Caroline."

As Bingley disappeared behind the door, Darcy steeled himself for the confrontation ahead, preparing to face whatever consequences their love might bring. But as he opened the door to his sister-in-law, he could not shake the feeling that this was the beginning of a much larger battle that would test the limits of their love and devotion.

"Caroline," he said, his voice steady despite the turmoil. "What can I do for you?"

"Fitzwilliam," she replied, her eyes searching his. "I believe we have much to discuss."

And with those ominous words, the chapter drew to a close, leaving readers on the edge of their seats, desperate to discover what fate had in store for Darcy and Bingley's passionate, forbidden love affair.

MR. DARCY PLEASURES HIMSELF

As the first rays of dawn delicately caressed the edges of Darcy's chamber window, he emerged from the realm of dreams. Yet, the ethereal allure of Charles Bingley clung to his consciousness with an intoxicating persistence. Once pristine and smooth, the fine linen sheets now entangled around his legs, indicating the passionate turmoil that had unfurled throughout the night. Within the intimate confines of his private bed chamber, the evidence of his arousal strained against the restraints of decency, a silent testament to the desires that stirred within him.

Driven by an irresistible force, Darcy's hands, muscular and sinewy, embarked upon a journey of self-discovery, tracing a path down his sculpted torso to the throbbing center of his desires. With a touch that spoke of familiarity, his fingers entwined themselves around the engorged member, eliciting a shudder of pleasure that coursed through his being. In the solitude of his chamber, the lines between fantasy and reality blurred as he conjured a vision of Bingley—the embodiment of grace and allure—his lithe form pressed against Darcy's own, their bodies melding in a symphony of passion.

In his mind, Darcy envisioned the tender surrender that awaited him, the exquisite dance of pleasure and intimacy that would bind their souls in an embrace beyond compare. The image of Bingley's supple frame, slightly smaller than his own, writhing with an unquenchable hunger, ignited a fire within him that burned with an intensity matched only by the sun's fiery ascent.

The climax, that long-awaited culmination of his fervent yearnings, approached with a swiftness that stole his breath away. With a gasp that echoed through the hallowed chambers, Darcy surrendered to the waves of ecstasy that crashed upon him, his essence spilling forth upon the expanse of his heaving, masculine chest. The release, as sweet as it was, left him both sated and yearning—for it was but a mere taste of what could be, of the depths of pleasure that lay unexplored between him and Bingley.

As the echoes of his desire reverberated within the chamber, Darcy lay spent, his body quivering with the remnants of ecstasy, his heart aflame with a hunger that refused to be quelled. The anticipation, the tantalizing prospect of what lay ahead, left him breathless, his soul yearning for the intoxicating connection that could exist between him and Bingley. For this was but the beginning, a prelude to a symphony of forbidden pleasures that awaited them both—an exquisite dance in which their bodies and souls would intertwine, defying the boundaries of a world that dared not speak their truth.

LATER THAT DAY, Darcy sought refuge in the peaceful solitude of his estate's lake. The sun cast a warm golden glow on the rippling water, and birds sang their melodies from the branches of the surrounding trees. Dressed in only an unbuttoned shirt and loose trousers, he eased himself into the small rowboat, leaving his shoes behind on the shore.

With each pull of the oars, Darcy felt the steady rhythm of his muscles working in harmony, propelling him further away from the world and closer to his thoughts. The beauty of nature enveloped him as if she were trying to soothe his troubled heart.

"Would that I could share this moment with you, Charles," Darcy whispered, his voice carrying across the gentle waves.

The serene atmosphere allowed Darcy's mind to wander back to his desires for Bingley. The thought of their bodies entwined, their lips locked in a passionate kiss, sent shivers down his spine despite the warmth of the sun on his skin. His heart ached with longing, and he couldn't help but wonder if Bingley shared in his desires.

"Only time will tell," Darcy murmured to himself, continuing to row across the lake, each stroke bringing him further into the embrace of solitude and the bittersweet fantasies of his heart's genuine desire.

As DARCY ROWED FURTHER into the lake, he spotted a secluded spot that seemed perfect for his needs. The area was shaded by a canopy of intertwining branches and leaves, providing a haven where he could be alone with his thoughts and desires. He guided the boat towards the hidden nook, needing to relieve himself as he entered the cool, sheltered space.

The boat came to rest gently against the soft moss-covered bank, and Darcy stood up, his eyes scanning the intimate surroundings. He felt a familiar stirring in his loins, a reminder of the fantasies that occupied his mind earlier that morning. With a deep exhale, he reached down to loosen his trousers, preparing to relieve himself.

As he stood there, the thick, long cock, twelve inches in length, was released from the confines of his trousers, bursting forth a steady stream of piss into the tranquil waters below. The liquid hitting the surface mingled with the gentle rustling of leaves above, creating an oddly soothing sensation.

Once finished, Darcy sighed contentedly, taking a moment to appreciate the privacy and intimacy of this hidden sanctuary. He could explore his feelings without fear or judgment, away from prying eyes. Tugging at his trousers, he pulled them down to the floor of the boat, sitting back on the wooden seat as he revealed his quickly engorged cock.

THE SIGHT of his arousal brought a flush to his cheeks, but he felt no shame in his desire. Instead, he reveled in the sensations coursing through him as he touched his throbbing length, each caress eliciting a fervent gasp from his lips. The world outside this secluded refuge ceased to exist, leaving only the intensity of his passion and the vivid imagery of Charles Bingley inhabiting his thoughts.

"Charles," he whispered, daring to speak the name aloud as his hand moved along his shaft, each stroke bringing him closer to the edge of ecstasy. The mere thought of being with Bingley sent shivers down his spine, causing his breath to hitch and his heart to race.

"Would that you were here," Darcy muttered, his voice barely audible above his panting. As he continued to touch himself, the words echoed through the secluded glade, a testament to the depth of his longing and the fire that burned within him.

DARCY'S MIND raced with visions of Charles Bingley as he stroked his engorged cock, each touch sending pleasure coursing through him. His body quivered with desire, the thought of Bingley's hands on him, his lips pressed against his own, fueling the fire within his loins.

"Charles," Darcy moaned, his voice breathless and full of yearning. "Oh, if you could only feel what I feel." He imagined the sight of Bingley before him, his golden curls framing his handsome face, a wicked grin playing upon his lips.

"Show me, Fitzwilliam," he heard Bingley's sultry voice say in his imagination. "Let me experience your desire."

The fantasy felt so real, as if Bingley were truly there with him, his presence palpable. Darcy's hand moved faster, his thumb grazing the sensitive head of his cock, sending shivers down his spine. The ache in his loins grew to unbearable heights, demanding release.

"TELL me how you want me, Fitzwilliam," Bingley whispered in his fantasy, his eyes alight with mischief and hunger. "Tell me how you would take me."

"Charles... I would kiss you until you could no longer breathe, until the world around us faded away," Darcy confessed, his voice trembling with need as he continued to touch himself. "I would explore every inch of your body, running my hands and lips over your smooth skin, leaving no part unclaimed."

"Then what?" Bingley's fantasy-self encouraged, his eyes shimmering with lust.

"Lower... I would move lower, taking your hardness into my mouth, tasting you, feeling you against my tongue," Darcy moaned as he imagined the exquisite pleasure of having Bingley in such a vulnerable position.

"Please, Fitzwilliam, don't stop there," begged the phantom Bingley, his cheeks flushed.

~

Darcy's breaths came in ragged gasps as he felt his climax approaching, the sensations building relentlessly within him. Desperate for more, he reached down with one hand, wetting his fingers with spit, and slowly began to pump it in and out of his ass. The unexpected intrusion sent his body reeling, and he imagined it was Bingley's tongue teasing him instead.

"Charles... if only you were here... I would let you take me, possess me, until we were both spent and sated," Darcy whispered hoarsely, his finger probing deeper as his hand on his cock moved faster, bringing him closer and closer to the edge.

"Then let us become one, Fitzwilliam," said the fantasy Bingley, his voice filled with passion and desire.

As the intensity of his desire built to an unbearable crescendo, Darcy could not hold back any longer. He cried out, his body shuddering as he spilled his seed, his orgasm consuming him like wildfire. His muscles clenched around his finger, the image of Bingley's tongue filling his mind, driving him to new heights of ecstasy.

~

Darcy gasped; the sensation of his finger buried deep inside him pushed him past the point of no return. "Charles!" he cried out, his voice filled with passion and desire as his body tensed and released in a powerful climax.

His seed erupted from his throbbing member, spattering against the boat's wooden floor, each pulse of pleasure shuddering through him like lightning. Darcy's mind was consumed by the thought of Bingley, the handsome man who had so effortlessly captured his heart and ignited his most primal desires.

"God, Charles," he panted, his breath coming in ragged gasps as the aftershocks of his orgasm pulsed through him. It was a moment of unadulterated pleasure and vulnerability, the likes of which he had never experienced before.

As the waves of ecstasy finally subsided, leaving him drained and spent, Darcy knew his life would never be the same again. He craved Bingley's touch with every fiber of his being and would stop at nothing to make their passionate union a reality.

SEX AT LUCAS LODGE

The evening ball, orchestrated with meticulous detail by the esteemed Sir William Lucas, unfolded within the splendid halls of Lucas Lodge, an embodiment of refined luxury. The air crackled with an electric vitality as the assembled guests' mingling voices intertwined with the orchestra's enchanting strains. Light and carefree laughter punctuated the symphony of music, casting a vibrant spell upon the festivities.

The grandeur of the occasion was evident in the attendees' attire, a visual spectacle that spoke volumes of their social standing and aspirations. The gentlemen, adorned in impeccably tailored waistcoats and breeches, strode with an air of confident elegance. Their garments, crafted from the finest fabrics, hinted at the wealth and refinement they possessed. The men wore extremely tight trousers, as current styles dictated, clearly outlining and exposing their many parts for all to see.

The ladies, no less captivating, graced the ballroom with an ethereal beauty, their gowns a tapestry of exquisite silks and satins that shimmered under the warm glow of countless candles. Each carefully selected and artfully embellished ensemble served as a meticulously crafted statement of their station and taste.

THE BALLROOM, adorned with gilded mirrors and crystal chandeliers, cast a spell upon its occupants, transporting them into a world of fleeting enchantment. The dance floor, a stage for the intricate choreography of social interactions, became a playground for whispered conversations and stolen glances. Courtly games of flirtation played out amidst the swirl of elegant gowns and the gentle clinking of champagne flutes. It was a theater of vanities, where both pride and desire vied for attention, a captivating dance of ambition and longing.

Amidst this opulent tapestry, Darcy and Bingley moved with grace and poise, commanding attention and respect. Their steps, meticulously measured, concealed the depths of their desires, yet their eyes, dark and smoldering, spoke a secret language known only to them. As they navigated the delicate intricacies of the ball, their gazes met in stolen moments, a silent affirmation of their connection, a flicker of a flame that burned too brightly to be extinguished.

For amid this glittering façade, hidden behind the layers of silk and satin, there existed a love that dared not speak its name. A love that defied the rigid constraints of society yet blossomed in the most clandestine corners of the heart. And as the night unfolded, amidst the laughter and music, amidst the shimmering gowns and well-tailored waistcoats, the world remained blissfully unaware of the passions that stirred within these two consenting gentlemen, destined to navigate the treacherous waters of desire and longing in a society that would frown upon their love.

DARCY ENTERED THE BALLROOM, his heart pounding in anticipation, knowing that Bingley would undoubtedly be present. He scanned the room, noting the various faces of high society mingling and conversing with one another. As much as he desired to locate Bingley, he knew appearances must be maintained. He engaged in polite conversation with those who approached him, his mind never straying far from the object of his desire.

"Mr. Darcy," Sir William Lucas greeted him warmly, "it is a pleasure to see you here tonight. I trust you are finding the company agreeable?"

"Indeed, Sir William," Darcy replied, his gaze flickering around the room as he searched for Bingley. "Your ball is a testament to your fine taste and hospitality."

"Ah, thank you, Mr. Darcy," Sir William said, his chest puffing up with pride. "I do so enjoy bringing people together for an evening of mirth and merriment."

"Your efforts are much appreciated," Darcy assured him, but inwardly, he could only think of one person with whom he wished to be brought together. And as the evening wore on, each moment spent without Bingley by his side felt like an eternity.

"Charles," he thought to himself, his heart racing and his breath catching in his throat, "where are you?"

DARCY'S ANTICIPATION grew as he searched for Bingley in the crowd, his heart racing with the possibility of seeing him again. The longing in his eyes was evident as they darted from one face to another, and his movements were tense and nervous.

The men at the ball wore tight waistcoats that hugged their chests, clearly displaying their well-defined physiques. Their smooth, high-waisted trousers left little to the imagination, fully exposing the contours of their crotches. For men of large endow-ments such as Darcy, hiding the size of their manhood was a near-impossible task in this new style of trousers. He tried to maintain an air of nonchalance, but it was difficult when so exposed and vulnerable.

"Mr. Darcy," a voice chimed in, causing him to lose focus on his quest to find Bingley momentarily. "A pleasure to see you here tonight."

"Ah, Lady Catherine," Darcy replied, forcing a smile as he turned to face her. "Likewise, I'm sure." His mind raced back to Bingley as soon as the brief exchange ended, his desire for the man consuming him.

Suddenly, amidst the sea of faces, Darcy finally spotted Bingley across the room, their eyes locking with an intensity that made his breath hitch. It felt as if an electric current surged between them, heightening their connection and making the rest of the room fade away.

BINGLEY'S EYES, like magnets drawn to a lodestone, remained firmly fixed upon the tantalizing contours of Darcy's trouser front, the bulge within becoming more pronounced with each passing moment. The heated intensity of Bingley's gaze ignited an inferno within Darcy, his body responding with an undeni-able ardor. A crimson blush crept upward, tainting his neck with a telltale flush, as a mingling of embarrassment and unquench-able desire coursed through his veins.

"Charles," Darcy's thoughts pleaded, his inner voice grap-pling for composure amidst the storm of sensations. "Must you test my resolve in this manner? Does the torment of temptation know no bounds?"

A swift exclamation, laden with warm familiarity, parted Bingley's lips, bridging the distance between them as he maneu-vered through the crowd of guests, his eyes locked steadfastly upon Darcy. The very sound of his name, uttered by Bingley's lips, sent tremors of anticipation rippling through Darcy's being.

"AH, MR. DARCY!" Bingley called out, his voice carrying the timbre of genuine delight. "What a fortuitous encounter this is! I am overjoyed to find you in attendance this evening."

Darcy's response, laced with a husky timbre, emerged in a low murmur, charged with a potent mixture of longing and restraint. "Charles, the pleasure is entirely mine."

Their proximity, exquisitely close, left little room for the imagination. The charged atmosphere thickened with an intoxicating blend of desire and unspoken yearning as if the very air conspired to draw them together. Their bodies stood on the precipice of contact, an electric tension that crackled between them, binding their souls in a clandestine dance of intimacy.

"May I suggest we take a walk outside, Mr. Darcy?" Bingley whispered into Darcy's ear, the warmth of his breath sending shivers down his spine.

His hushed proposal was whispered with a breathy intensity. Slipping from Bingley's lips, the warmth of his breath grazed Darcy's ear, sending shivers cascading down his spine. Darcy nodded silently, his voice momentarily abandoned by the surge of emotions that held him captive. Together, they disentangled themselves from the crowded dance floor, their fingers grazing against one another in a tantalizing brush as they set toward the beckoning allure of the moonlit garden.

THE NIGHT AIR was cool and refreshing, a welcome reprieve from the oppressive atmosphere. The moonlight illuminated the garden, casting an ethereal glow on the blooming flowers and lush foliage surrounding them. A gentle breeze rustled through the trees, carrying the sweet scent of jasmine.

As they walked, Darcy admired how Bingley's golden curls bounced lightly against the nape of his neck, longing to bury his fingers in them. His eyes roamed over Bingley's smaller frame, taking in the curve of his shoulders, the swell of his chest beneath his waistcoat, and the subtle dip at his lower back where the high-waisted trousers hugged his body just so.

"Such a beautiful night," Bingley remarked, his gaze meeting Darcy's. "And even more beautiful company."

Darcy felt heat rush to his cheeks, his heart racing at the compliment. As they strolled further, the laughter and music from inside grew fainter, enveloping the two men in a cocoon of intimacy.

"Over here," Bingley suggested, leading Darcy towards a secluded corner of the garden hidden by a tall hedge. Here, they were protected from prying eyes, free to let their desires run wild.

"Charles," Darcy murmured as he took Bingley into his arms, their bodies pressed tightly together. Their lips met in a passionate kiss, tongues dancing together in a sensual rhythm that echoed the beat of their hearts.

BINGLEY'S HANDS grasped Darcy's broad shoulders, pulling him closer as their mouths devoured each other with an urgency that betrayed their longing. Between them, Darcy could feel the hardness in Bingley's trousers growing, pressing against his throbbing erection.

"God, Fitzwilliam," Bingley gasped into his mouth, his fingers digging into Darcy's biceps. "I have wanted this all week. I have thought of nothing else."

"Me too," Darcy confessed, his voice thick with desire. "Every time I close my eyes, all I can think about is touching you, tasting you...possessing you."

"Then possess me," Bingley urged, his eyes dark and hungry. "Right here, right now."

The intensity of their connection was like a flame igniting within them, unstoppable and all-consuming. They gave themselves to it, surrendering to the passion that threatened to consume them. With every heated touch, every shuddering breath, they knew that nothing would ever be the same.

"Let me," Darcy whispered, his fingers trembling slightly as they reached for the waistband of Bingley's satin trousers. The anticipation was palpable between them, a magnetic force that seemed to draw their bodies closer together even as they attempted to undress.

Bingley mirrored Darcy's movements, showcasing his desire through the urgency of his touch. As they slowly loosened each other's belts and unbuttoned the tight waists, their breaths came in short, shallow gasps mingling in the air between them.

"Charles, I cannot wait any longer," Darcy confessed, his voice thick with arousal as he slid Bingley's trousers down his lean thighs, exposing the taut muscles and silky skin beneath. As he revealed more and more of Bingley's body, he couldn't help but let out a moan of appreciation at the sight of his lover's engorged cock, barely restrained by the delicate fabric of his undergarments.

"Neither can I, Fitzwilliam," Bingley replied, echoing Darcy's impatience as he lowered Darcy's trousers. His fingers brushed against the bulging outline of Darcy's erection, eliciting a shiver from both men.

FINALLY FREE OF their constricting clothing, Darcy and Bingley stood before one another, fully exposed and vulnerable. Yet there was no fear or hesitation in their eyes, only an intense, shared craving that burned hotter than the sun above them.

"Touch me," Bingley urged, reaching for Darcy's hand and guiding it towards his throbbing length. "Please."

Darcy obliged, wrapping his fingers around Bingley's cock and stroking him slowly, exploring every ridge and vein with a curious, respectful touch. At the same time, Bingley mirrored his actions, grasping Darcy's erection with a firm, possessive grip.

"Ah, Charles," Darcy moaned, his head falling back as he surrendered to the pleasure of Bingley's touch. "Your hands are like heaven."

"Yours too, Fitzwilliam," Bingley panted, his eyes fluttering closed as they began to move in unison, their strokes gradually increasing in speed and pressure.

AS THEIR RHYTHM INTENSIFIED, so did the sensations coursing through their bodies. Every nerve ending seemed to be on fire, every breath they took was laced with desire, and every beat of their hearts throbbed in time with the strokes of their hands.

"Charles, I am coming close to my orgasm," Darcy admitted, his voice barely more than a ragged whisper as he felt the pleasure building inside him, threatening to consume him whole.

"Me too, Fitzwilliam," Bingley gasped, his grip on Darcy's cock tightening as if trying to hold back the impending tide.

"Let's explode together," Darcy suggested, his free hand reaching out to entwine with Bingley's. "Together, Charles."

"Agreed," Bingley managed, his body shuddering with need. "Now, Fitzwilliam, now!"

And so, with one final, synchronized stroke, Darcy and Bingley reached the peak of their passionate climb. Their cries echoed throughout the secluded garden, a testament to their profound connection, a bond forged in the heat and intensity of their mutual desire.

~

AFTER THEIR MUTUAL CLIMAX, Darcy and Bingley stood trembling, holding each other for support as their breathing slowly returned to normal. The intensity of their shared pleasure was unlike anything they had ever experienced, leaving them both physically sated yet emotionally charged.

"Charles," Darcy whispered into Bingley's ear, his voice quivering with emotion. "What we shared...I never knew such a connection could exist between two people."

"Neither did I," Bingley admitted, pressing his lips tenderly against Darcy's neck. "Fitzwilliam, I cannot deny my powerful attraction for you. It is as though our souls were destined to intertwine."

"Destiny or not," Darcy murmured, running his fingers through Bingley's soft curls, "I am wholly captivated by you."

A moment of silence passed between them, filled only by the sounds of their beating hearts and gentle breaths. Then, with regret, Darcy reluctantly pulled away from Bingley's embrace.

~

"I FEAR we must return to the ball," he said, his eyes conveying his longing. "But know that I shall think of this every moment we are apart."

"Agreed," Bingley replied, his face reflecting a similar sense of loss. "But Fitzwilliam, promise me something."

"Anything, Charles."

"Promise me that this is only the beginning of our story," Bingley implored, his gaze full of hope and desire. "Promise me that we will find a way to be together, no matter the obstacles we face."

Darcy captured Bingley's hand in his own, bringing it to his lips and kissing it gently. "I promise, Charles. Though society may frown upon our love, I will do everything possible to ensure our happiness."

"Then let us face the future together," Bingley declared, his eyes shining with determination. "Side by side, hand in hand."

"Hand in hand," Darcy echoed, sealing their vow with a tender kiss.

REDRESSING EACH OTHER, the two handsome and sexually spent gentlemen reluctantly returned to the festivities, the lingering warmth of their shared passion burning within them, a beacon of hope amidst the uncertainty of their lives. And though they could not yet foresee the challenges ahead, they were determined to overcome them, united by a love that would not be denied.

For now, however, they had only the stolen moments, the secretive glances, and furtive touches to sustain them. But as they moved through the crowded ballroom, surrounded by the trappings of society and propriety, the intensity of their connection could not be contained. For every brief brush of fingertips against a thigh, each knowing smile exchanged, and every whispered word of desire was a testament to their growing bond, a reminder of the depth of their love and the strength it gave them.

With each passing day, Darcy and Bingley were becoming more entwined, their passion growing stronger and more profound. And so, despite their challenges, they clung to their promise to one another, driven by an unwavering belief in their love and the certainty that they could overcome any obstacle together.

THE GARDENER'S PLEASURE

Darcy's eyes fluttered open, greeted by the soft embrace of the sumptuous bed linens that lovingly cradled his form. A surge of awareness coursed through his veins, his heart echoing with a relentless rhythm that matched the cadence of his thoughts— thoughts consumed entirely by the magnetic pull of Bingley. The tendrils of their shared desire had woven a tapestry too intricate to ignore, binding them in a web of longing that defied the boundaries of societal expectations.

Rising from the bed, his body still thrumming with the echoes of passion, Darcy moved with purpose across the expanse of his boudoir, the cool marble beneath his feet a stark contrast to the heat that radiated from his core. His strides carried an air of determination, driven by an understanding he could no longer deny—a truth that whispered through his veins, demanding acknowledgment.

Approaching the window, Darcy's eyes were bathed in the golden embrace of the morning sun, casting a warm glow upon his sculpted physique, accentuating the contours of his muscular frame. The ethereal light danced upon his bare skin, tracing pathways of warmth that mirrored the fire that burned within him.

~

As HIS GAZE descended upon the garden below, a tableau of nature's beauty unfolded before him—an orchestrated symphony of flora and fauna. Young gardeners, their lithe forms adorned in well-worn garments, toiled diligently amidst the verdant landscape. Beads of sweat glistened upon their brows, their bodies honed by hard work and the summer sun, a sight that stirred a wicked thought within Darcy's mind, an undeniable urge that beckoned him to indulge in the depths of his desires.

One particular gardener, blessed with a countenance that mirrored a Greek god's sculpted perfection, commanded Darcy's attention. His jawline, chiseled as if hewn from marble, framed a visage of arresting beauty—a symphony of masculine allure that captivated Darcy's gaze. Eyes, deep and penetrating, seemed to hold secrets untold, drawing Darcy into their depths with an intoxicating charm.

Temptation coursed through Darcy's veins, an irresistible invitation to revel in the passions that lay just beyond the boundaries of propriety. The air crackled with the forbidden possibilities, and Darcy, ever the master of his fate, succumbed to the call of his desires—a clandestine dance that promised pleasures yet unexplored.

For the garden would bear witness to a union forged in the crucible of unbridled passion, where the boundaries of expectation would be shattered, giving way to the intoxicating liberation that only genuine desire could bestow.

FULLY EXPOSED on his balcony for all to see, Darcy's two hands found their way to his fully engorged twelve-inch cock, already throbbing with need. He began to stroke himself, his breath hitching as he watched the young gardener work. It was not long before the gardener glanced up, his eyes meeting Darcy's in a moment of shared desire. As Darcy continued to pleasure himself, the gardener's smile broadened with each stroke, fueling his lust. The gardener reached into his pants and started stroking his cock in rhythm with Darcy, fast and furious in his attempt to explode with his master.

Unable to contain himself any longer, Darcy exploded, streams of cum bursting forth from his rigid member and arcing out toward the gardener below. The young man smiled as he, too, dumped a load of cum into his pants, nodding to Darcy in acknowledgment before returning to his task. Darcy leaned against the window frame, momentarily sated but all too aware that his genuine desire lay elsewhere.

"Damn these societal expectations," he muttered under his breath, torn between his growing feelings for Bingley and the constraints of propriety. "Can I truly allow myself this happiness, knowing the scandal it may cause?"

In the quiet of his chamber, Darcy wrestled with his conscience, his heart heavy with longing and uncertainty. The thought of Bingley's touch set his mind ablaze, yet he knew that pursuing their desires would risk the reputations they had both worked so hard to maintain.

"Is it worth it?" he whispered, desperate for guidance in a world that offered none. "Can I truly sacrifice everything for the sake of love?"

As the sun continued to rise, Darcy was left to ponder his decision, the echoes of his inner turmoil haunting him as the day began.

≈

"ENOUGH," Darcy murmured, determination surging through his veins. "I cannot deny who I am any longer." With a newfound resolve, he decided to pursue his feelings for Bingley, come what may.

For generations, Pemberley, the grand estate in Darcy's family, was ripe with hidden nooks and crannies perfect for secret rendezvous. The manor house stood tall and imposing, its elegant architecture a testament to the wealth and status of its occupants. The gardens, a lush Eden of vibrant flowers and verdant foliage, provided ample cover for those seeking solace from prying eyes.

"Charles Bingley," Darcy whispered, his breath hitching at the mere mention of the man's name. He could not help but think of the smaller gentleman, with his curly blond hair pulled back into a loose ponytail, and how his laughter seemed to light up a room. Oh, how he longed to be in Bingley's company once more, to feel the warmth of his touch and the heat of their bodies entwined.

"By God, I want him," Darcy confessed to himself as he paced the length of the drawing-room, the plush carpet beneath his feet doing little to ease his restless energy. "And if I must defy society to have him, then so be it."

HE IMAGINED meeting Bingley within one of Pemberley's many secluded alcoves, their eyes locking with an intensity that spoke volumes before a single word was uttered. The thrill of such an encounter sent shivers down Darcy's spine, his body tingling with anticipation.

"Are you ready for this?" he would ask, his voice low and husky with desire.

"More than anything," Bingley would reply, the unbridled passion in his eyes rendering further words unnecessary.

"Then let us begin," Darcy would say, taking Bingley's hand

and leading him deeper into the shadows of Pemberley's hidden world.

He imagined their journey through the dimly lit corridors, their steps hushed by the thick velvet drapes that lined the walls. In quiet corners, they would pause to steal furtive kisses, each one more vibrant than the last as their lust threatened to consume them.

"Darling," Bingley would murmur between breaths, his eyes glistening with unshed tears. "I never knew it could be like this."

"Nor did I," Darcy would reply, his heart swelling with love and gratitude for the man who had shown him what true happiness felt like.

In the privacy of their secret sanctuary, Darcy envisioned their bodies entwined, skin slick with sweat as they explored each other's every curve and crevice. The taste of Bingley's lips, the feel of his muscular thighs wrapped around Darcy's waist – these images filled his mind, driving him to the brink of madness with want.

"Please," he begged inwardly, desperate for release from the torment of his unfulfilled desires. "Let our love be enough to overcome the obstacles that lie ahead."

Darcy made a silent vow: no matter what challenges awaited them, he would fight tooth and nail to ensure he and Bingley could share a life filled with passion, love, and understanding.

A SECRET RETREAT

~

D
arcy stood amidst the solitude of the forsaken outbuilding, his gaze drawn to the weathered wooden door that stood as a sentinel, separating him from the outside world. The stagnant and heavy air clung to the small structure, perfumed with the earthy scent of ancient hay and the lingering essence of damp wood. Yet, to Darcy, it was a sanctuary, a haven where he could cast off the shackles of societal expectations and reveal his true self, unencumbered by judgment or censure.

Within the confines of that humble refuge, Darcy's heart fluttered with palpable anticipation, its rhythm echoing in his ears like the distant roll of thunder heralding an approaching storm. Like wild horses, his thoughts galloped through the corridors of his mind, desperately seeking answers to the questions that tormented him. Would Bingley come? Did Bingley share the same yearning that burned with an unquenchable fervor within Darcy's chest? The uncertainty, like a fog that clung to his thoughts, mingled with the excitement that coursed through his veins.

Restless, Darcy paced the uneven stone floor, his footsteps

marking the passage of time with a rhythmic cadence. In his mind's eye, he conjured images of their previous encounters— their stolen moments of intimacy that ignited a flame within him. The memory of tender touches, gentle and electrifying, danced before him. The remembrance of stolen glances, laden with unspoken desires, played like a silent film across the canvas of his imagination. And the unuttered words, heavy with meaning, lingered between them, suspended like whispers in the wind, begging to be acknowledged.

"PLEASE, PLEASE," Darcy silently implored, his fingers curling into tight fists at his sides, a testament to the intensity of his yearning. "Let him come to me. Let him share in this clandestine meeting that consumes my every thought and fills my nights with restless longing."

In that small, forgotten space, Darcy stood as a vessel of hope, his heart a beacon that called out to Bingley, reaching across the vast expanse of their shared desires. As the air within the outbuilding hung heavy with possibilities, he found solace in the belief that Bingley, too, felt the magnetic pull of their connection and that he, too, yearned for the forbidden pleasures that awaited them.

Thus, Darcy stood, poised on the precipice of destiny, his breath catching in his throat, as he awaited the arrival of the one who could unlock the secrets of his heart and set ablaze the passions that burned within them both.

THE DOOR TO THE SMALL, forsaken outbuilding creaked open, its rusty hinges groaning in protest against the passage of time. Like a curtain parting on a theatrical stage, it revealed a tableau bathed in the resplendent hues of the setting sun, casting long, ephemeral shadows that danced upon the dusty floor. And there, framed by the warm, golden glow, stood Bingley—a figure of vulnerability and determination. His eyes, broad and uncertain, mirrored the flickering flames of a thousand emotions, while his body, taut with restrained longing, yearned to bridge the distance that separated them.

"Charles," Darcy whispered, his voice a fragile thread of sound, laden with the weight of unspoken depths, as he traversed the room with purposeful strides. Once an insurmountable expanse, the space between them diminished instantly as they were drawn together by a gravitational force too powerful to resist. Their eyes, twin pools of understanding, locked in an unbreakable gaze, and at that moment, doubt dissipated, vanishing like mist before the sun's rays.

Their bodies melded seamlessly, like two halves of a long-lost whole, as they succumbed to the magnetic pull that had bound them since their first fateful encounter. In the embrace of their shared desires, the world outside ceased to exist, leaving only the sanctuary of their union, where time stood still.

"God, Darcy," Bingley breathed against the curve of Darcy's neck, his voice a tender exhalation, trembling with a mixture of awe and longing. His fingers, possessed by an urgency born of desire, gripped Darcy's shoulders with fervor as if seeking an anchor in the storm of their emotions. "I did not know if you would truly be here. I feared that perhaps I had imagined it all, that the intensity of my feelings had deceived me."

Darcy's response, a declaration etched upon their shared air, resounded with unwavering conviction. "Every moment we have shared, Charles, has been indelibly etched into the very fabric of my heart. The mere thought of denying these feelings, of stifling this connection, is an agony I can no longer bear."

Bingley's admission, raw and vulnerable, spilled forth with a tremor in his voice as he met Darcy's unwavering gaze. "Nor can I, Darcy. I have been plagued by doubts, haunted by the fear that you might change your mind or, worse yet, that you had never truly felt what I feel for you."

A gentle caress, tender and reassuring, accompanied Darcy's response, his fingers brushing away a stray tendril of golden hair that had fallen upon Bingley's flushed cheek. "Never doubt my love for you, Charles. It burns as brightly as the sun, as steadfast as the North Star. I would traverse the depths of hell or ascend the highest peaks of heaven to be with you. Consequences be damned, for love knows no boundaries."

In that sacred moment, their bond forged in the crucible of shared desire was sealed, and they stood united, two souls intertwined against the backdrop of a world they might never understand. Their love, a clandestine flame that defied the strictures of society, blazed with an intensity that would illuminate their path, guiding them through the labyrinth of obstacles that lay ahead. Together, they would navigate the treacherous waters of longing and liberation, hand in hand, their spirits entwined in a dance of unyielding devotion.

As THEIR LIPS met in a searing kiss, the world outside seemed to fade away, leaving only the two of them locked in a dance as old as time. And though they knew that the path ahead would be fraught with peril and heartache, they also recognized the beauty of the love they had found – a love that transcended societal norms and defied the expectations of those who would seek to tear them apart.

For now, in this hidden corner of Pemberley, they were free to be themselves, explore the depths of their passion, and bask in the glow of a love that burned brighter than the sun.

As Darcy held Bingley close, he could feel the intensity of their connection radiating through every fiber of his being. It was as if they were two souls destined to meet, drawn together by some unseen force that defied logic and reason. Their eyes locked, and at that moment, Darcy felt a sense of vulnerability he had never experienced before.

"Charles," Darcy whispered, his voice trembling with emotion. "I have longed for this moment since we first met."

"Your words echo my own thoughts, Fitzwilliam," Bingley replied, tears welling up in his expressive blue eyes. He leaned into Darcy's embrace, allowing himself to be consoled by the strong arms that encircled him. "I have dreamed of us together, but I never dared hope it could become a reality."

"Neither did I," Darcy admitted, feeling profound gratitude for the love they could share. He pressed his lips tenderly against Bingley's forehead, tasting the salt of his tears. "But we are here now, and we must seize the opportunity fate has presented us."

"THEN, let us not waste another precious moment," Bingley declared, his voice resonating with a potent blend of unwavering resolve and fervent desire. His gaze, reflecting their shared longing, shimmered with an intensity that promised to set their world ablaze.

With an almost reverential slowness, they embarked upon the task of unveiling each other's hidden forms. Darcy's fingers quivered with anticipation as he delicately undid the buttons of Bingley's waistcoat, revealing the pristine expanse of fine linen beneath its tailored exterior. Likewise, Bingley's hands mirrored the tremors of his lover's touch as he gingerly loosened Darcy's cravat, allowing it to slither away like a discarded serpent's skin.

"Forgive me, Fitzwilliam," Bingley murmured, his voice a soft confession of vulnerability, as his nimble fingers faltered in their pursuit of unbuttoning Darcy's shirt. "My hands have conspired against me, refusing to heed my command."

Darcy's response, tender and understanding, came in a gentle reassurance. "Fear not, my dearest Charles. Allow me the honor of assisting you in this endeavor." Taking the lead, he assumed the role of the gentle conductor, guiding their shared symphony of undressing. With each button that surrendered to his touch, a tremor of anticipation coursed through his veins, electrifying the air between them.

THE SIGHT of Bingley's bared chest, adorned with a tantalizing dusting of golden hair and sculpted with firm, sinewy contours, ignited a fervent flame within Darcy's core, sending a thrilling shiver down his spine.

Now, the time had come for their roles to be reversed. With a voice hushed and laden with tender affection, Darcy stepped back, granting Bingley the freedom to peel away the layers that concealed his muscular and hairy form. Their fingers brushed against each other's skin, the gentle contact sparking a delirious inferno that threatened to consume them both. In that fleeting touch, they discovered a language beyond words—a language of heat and longing, of unspoken promises and uncharted territories.

As the fabric yielded and their bodies were unveiled, they stood before each other, bare and exposed in their shared vulnerability. In that moment, the world around them dissolved into insignificance, for they had embarked upon a sacred journey of exploration, trust, and unadulterated passion. Their desire was woven with threads of tenderness and ardent yearning, with every touch, every caress, kindling a flame that would burn brighter with each passing moment.

HAND IN HAND, they embarked upon the delicate task of disrobing, their movements synchronized perfectly. Each garment shed was a symbolic barrier dismantled, a societal expectation cast aside as they ventured further into their shared desires. With every layer that fell away, the air grew heavy with anticipation, charged with an electric current that pulsed between them.

And so, they stood before one another, clothed only in their breeches—their vulnerability and trust were complete. Lowering their breeches allowed them finally to become one. Becoming two fully naked men together was as intense as it was sincere. The room seemed to hold its breath, the walls bearing witness to the profound intimacy that unfolded within its confines. Hearts raced in tandem, their beats echoing the rhythm of their mutual longing.

"Darcy," he exhaled, his voice a fragile whisper, his gaze enraptured by the undeniable evidence of Bingley's arousal, straining against the confines of his breeches. "Never have I yearned for anyone more fervently than I yearn for you now."

Bingley's response was a testament to the depths of his desire, his voice heavy with both need and surrender. "And I, Fitzwilliam. No force in this world can rival the intensity of my longing for you. Let us cast aside our fears and inhibitions and surrender ourselves to the intoxicating pleasures that await."

WITH A SHARED UNDERSTANDING, their hands moved in unison. In the soft glow of the candlelight, their skin became a canvas imbued with warmth and luminescence, every contour and sinew accentuated by the interplay of light and shadow.

Darcy's chest was broad and commanding, communicating his strength and power, while a mesmerizing cascade of dark curls adorned his pectorals, inviting touch and exploration. Equally endowed with a physique of masculine beauty, Bingley exuded a radiance enhanced by the golden tresses gracing his robust form. Together, they were a tableau of masculine grace, their bodies testaments to the allure and magnetism that bound them in this sacred union.

The world outside ceased to exist. They were no longer constrained by the expectations and conventions that governed their lives. Instead, they were free to explore the depths of their desires and revel in the exquisite pleasure that awaited them. And as their bodies stood intertwined, bathed in the tender glow of the flickering candlelight, they knew they had embarked upon a journey that would forever alter the course of their hearts and souls.

"CHARLES," Darcy breathed, his voice a tantalizing murmur that danced upon the air, "the sight of your body is nothing short of magnificent." With a gentle touch, his fingertips traced the sinewy contours of Bingley's abdomen, following the lines of his muscles with an almost reverent reverence. The caress, feather-light yet laden with a promise of pleasure, elicited a hitch in Bingley's breath, his arousal mounting in response to the intimate exploration.

"Your words humble me, Fitzwilliam," Bingley replied, his voice a soft confession of admiration and desire. His hands, emboldened by a growing hunger, embarked upon an odyssey of discovery, tracing the firm ridges of Darcy's chest, and mapping the terrain of masculine beauty before him.

As the boundaries of restraint blurred and their yearning became insatiable, the magnetic pull between them became undeniable. Succumbing to their shared longing, Darcy pressed his lips against Bingley's, their mouths melding in a fervent union. Their tongues danced with an intoxicating rhythm, an intricate choreography of passion and desire that left no doubt of their shared hunger. All else faded into insignificance, for the intoxicating allure of each other consumed them.

NO LONGER CONTENT with mere exploration, their hands sought a more primal connection. Fingers tightened, digging into the hardened muscles beneath the surface, each touch a testament to their mutual craving. The symphony of their desire played out in the language of touch, a sensual melody that resonated through their bodies and kindled a fire that threatened to consume them both.

Yet, amidst the fervor of their longing, Darcy's touch found purpose. With a deliberate motion, he reached for the small vial of oil he had thoughtfully brought along, anticipating the need for this moment of consummation. It was a tender gesture, an unspoken promise of care and preparation, an acknowledgment of the heights of pleasure they were about to ascend.

"Are you ready, Charles?" Darcy's voice, a mere breath upon his lover's ear, carried a question of consent that held the weight of trust and vulnerability.

Bingley's response was immediate, his voice laden with anticipation and longing. "More than ready, Fitzwilliam. With every fiber of my being, I yearn for this union of our souls."

In his eyes, Darcy saw the reflection of trust and desire, a silent affirmation that ignited a flame of passion within his own heart. And so, guided by their shared longing and the unyielding bond, they embarked upon a journey that would forever alter the fabric of their lives, exploring pleasure and intimacy that would leave an indelible mark upon their souls.

DARCY POURED a generous amount of oil onto his fingers and gently massaged it into Bingley's eager and gaping hole, ensuring he would be well-prepared for what was to come. Bingley's breaths became shallow, anticipation and a hint of nervousness mingling.

"Relax, my love," Darcy murmured, tenderly kissing Bingley's forehead. "I promise to be gentle."

Bingley nodded, closing his eyes as he leaned into Darcy's embrace. As Darcy coated his throbbing cock with the slick oil, he could not help but marvel at the sight before him. Bingley's body, flushed with desire and bathed in the warm candlelight, was a vision of erotic beauty.

"Are you certain, Charles?" Darcy asked once more, positioning himself at Bingley's entrance.

"Please, Fitzwilliam," Bingley pleaded, his voice laden with need. "I want this."

With a firm nod, Darcy slowly pushed forward, entering Bingley with great care and attention to his reactions. Bingley's face contorted in pain and pleasure as he accommodated Darcy's impressive girth.

"TAKE ALL the time you need, my love," Darcy whispered, his voice a tender caress that carried the weight of patience and understanding. He willed himself to remain still, to grant Bingley the space and time to adjust to the new sensations that enveloped them both. The promise of an entire night stretched before them, a canvas upon which they could paint their desires with brushstrokes of tenderness and passion.

As Bingley's breathing gradually steadied, and the initial tension in his body began to yield to a sense of surrender, Darcy guided their connection further. With measured care, he pressed on, inch by deliberate inch, until he was fully sheathed within his lover. The overwhelming warmth and exquisitely tight embrace threatened to consume him, unraveling the control threads that held him in check. Yet, for Bingley's sake, he remained steadfast, maintaining a steady rhythm that allowed them to explore this new realm of intimacy together.

"More," Bingley gasped, his voice a plea that echoed through the room, his fingers gripping Darcy's arms with a fervor born of desire. "Please, Fitzwilliam, grant me the depth of your love. I yearn for more of you, to be united in body and soul."

Darcy's heart swelled at the raw need in Bingley's eyes, a need that mirrored his own. With a lover's devotion, he obliged, pulling back and thrusting gently into Bingley, their bodies finding a rhythm that echoed the symphony of their shared desire. Panting breaths mingled in the air, punctuated by the intoxicating melody of moans and gasps, as pleasure surged and surged again, threatening to engulf them both in its tumultuous waves.

THE INITIAL PAIN and discomfort that had accompanied their union gradually yielded to a crescendo of pleasure, an exquisite dance of sensations that left them teetering on the precipice of ecstasy. Wave after wave crashed upon them, their bodies moving in perfect synchrony, slick with the sheen of sweat and the essence of their shared intimacy. With every thrust and arch of their bodies against one another, they drew closer to the pinnacle of their desires.

Their eyes, locked in an unbreakable gaze, spoke volumes of the love and ardor that burned between them. In that intimate exchange of glances, they found solace and reassurance, a silent understanding that their union transcended mere physicality. It was a union of hearts and souls, an affirmation of their connection that eclipsed the boundaries of societal expectations and conventions.

And so, they surrendered themselves wholly to the rhythm of their bodies, to the symphony of their desires. In the flickering candlelight, their forms intertwined; they became one with the depth of their love and the unyielding bond that would forever bind them together.

"CHARLES," Darcy breathed, his voice filled with a heady mix of urgency and anticipation, his body teetering on the precipice of release. "I fear I can no longer resist the overwhelming tide of pleasure that engulfs me."

Bingley, in turn, felt his climax imminent, his body aflame with desire. He met Darcy's gaze, their eyes locking in a shared understanding. "Neither can I, Fitzwilliam," he confessed, his voice a breathless admission of need. "Let us journey together, find our ultimate pleasure in one another's embrace."

With an almost desperate fervor, Darcy mustered his remaining strength, his final thrust carrying them both over the edge into a realm of exquisite ecstasy. Their voices, entwined in a duet of passion, reverberated through the hidden chamber, their cries of pleasure mingling with the air, an ode to the consummation of their desires.

As the waves of sensation gradually subsided, Darcy and Bingley were entwined in the aftermath of their intense love-making. Their bodies trembled with the aftershocks of pleasure, their breathing steadying progressively as they navigated the fragile space between satiation and contentment.

"CHARLES," Darcy murmured, his voice a velvety caress, as he gently kissed Bingley's lips. The touch was tender, an unspoken promise of love and devotion that lingered in the air. "As our hearts beat as one, I am filled with an overwhelming love for you —a love that knows no bounds."

Bingley's eyes, shining with unshed tears of joy, met Darcy's gaze with a depth of emotion mirrored his own. "And I,

Fitzwilliam," he replied, his voice filled with a quiet certainty. "No matter what trials may lie ahead, know that my heart will forever belong to you. I find solace, strength, and a love that surpasses all measure in your arms."

In the hushed stillness of the chamber, they lay intertwined, their bodies a testament to the profound connection they shared. Once hidden and forbidden, their love blossomed in the face of adversity, defying societal expectations and conventions. And as they basked in the afterglow of their union, they knew that their hearts, forever entwined, would weather any storm that fate may cast upon them.

STILL JOINED with his cock placed within Bingley's ass, the two men lay entwined within the softly lit chamber, their bodies a testament to the intensity of their shared passion. The room hummed with an ethereal energy, heavy with the lingering scent of their desire and the warmth of their entangled limbs.

Concern etched Darcy's features as he gazed into Bingley's eyes, his voice a gentle murmur that carried the weight of his love. "Did I cause you pain, my dearest Charles?" he inquired, his fingers tenderly caressing Bingley's cheek, seeking solace in the familiar curves of his beloved's face.

A tender smile graced Bingley's lips, a testament to the depth of their connection, as he shook his head, his voice imbued with unwavering devotion. "No, Fitzwilliam, any fleeting discomfort was inconsequential in the face of our profound love. The pleasure you bestow upon me far outweighs any momentary ache."

Relief washed over Darcy, his features softening with a profound tenderness. He brushed aside stray curls from Bingley's forehead, his fingertips lingering in the golden strands as if savoring the intimate touch. "You must know, my love, that causing you pain would be anathema to my very being. Your happiness and well-being are the cornerstones of my existence."

~

BINGLEY'S VOICE, rich with desire and affection, enveloped the space between them, a sultry whisper that ignited the embers of their shared passion. "Your touch, Fitzwilliam, it sets me ablaze with a fervor that defies description. It engulfs me, ignites the very essence of my soul. I have never experienced such pleasure nor known a love so profound."

Darcy's heart swelled within his chest, a wave of vulnerability washing over him as he bared his emotions. "Nor have I, Charles," he confessed, his voice laced with awe and vulnerability. "In your presence, the world fades into insignificance. There is only you, our love, and the sanctuary we have constructed within the shelter of one another's hearts."

Bingley's lips, warm against Darcy's neck, brushed delicate kisses along the expanse of his skin, the gesture a testament to their intimate connection. He inhaled deeply, savoring Darcy's intoxicating scent, a fragrance that stirred his senses and anchored him to their shared reality. "May this bond never falter," he murmured, his words a fervent prayer. "Fitzwilliam, I cannot fathom a life devoid of your presence. You are my sun, moon, and stars guiding me through the darkest nights."

~

"CHARLES," Darcy choked out, feeling tears prick at the corners of his eyes. Never before had he allowed himself to be so vulnerable, but he knew that Bingley was worth every ounce of fear and uncertainty. "Promise me, no matter what obstacles we face, that our love will remain strong and true."

"Of course, my love," Bingley said with conviction, his gaze fierce and unwavering. "I promise you, Fitzwilliam Darcy, that my heart will be forever yours."

"Then let us seal our vows with a kiss," Darcy whispered, capturing Bingley's lips in a tender, yet passionate, embrace.

As their mouths met, their bodies pressed together, the last remnants of their previous passion still clinging to their heated skin. Each brush of their fingers against one another's flesh was a testament to their love – a silent affirmation that they belonged to each other entirely.

"Sleep now, Charles," Darcy murmured, kissing Bingley's forehead gently. "For tomorrow, we begin anew, fortified by our love and devotion."

"Until then, Fitzwilliam," Bingley whispered, closing his eyes and nestling into Darcy's embrace. "Until then."

And so, hand in hand, heart to heart, Darcy and Bingley drifted off to sleep, secure in the knowledge that their love would endure.

THOMAS BERTRAM, SEX TUTOR

The sun dipped low on the horizon, casting a warm, ethereal glow that painted the drawing-room windows in hues of orange and pink. A tempest of emotions consumed Fitzwilliam Darcy within this intimate setting, his countenance reflecting the inner turmoil within his heart. His connection with Charles Bingley had deepened, their bond growing increasingly intimate, yet a persistent haze of uncertainty clouded Darcy's mind—a longing for guidance and clarity tugging at his soul.

Restlessly, Darcy paced back and forth across the room, his steps measured but agitated. His brow furrowed, a testament to the intensity of his contemplation, as he grappled with the questions that plagued him. The flickering candlelight cast dancing shadows upon his features, accentuating the lines of worry etched upon his face.

"Confusion plagues my every thought," Darcy muttered under his breath, his exhalations fogging up the windowpane as he gazed longingly into the distance, seeking solace in the beauty of the rolling countryside. "I must find a way to unravel the intricacies of these feelings that consume me."

~

As if summoned by Darcy's inner plea, Thomas Bertram, a dear friend and confidant, entered the drawing room. His tall and lithe form, draped in the fashionable attire of the era, was framed by the doorway, an embodiment of refined elegance. The flickering candlelight cast a soft glow upon his features, illuminating the strong lines of his face and the mischievous glint in his dark eyes.

"Ah, Darcy," Thomas said, his voice a deep timbre that resonated through the room, "I had hoped to find you here. It appears that your thoughts mirror my restless musings."

Darcy's troubled gaze met Thomas's, a glimmer of hope flickering within his eyes. The presence of his dear friend offered a respite, a chance to share the burden that weighed heavily upon his heart. With a mixture of trepidation and eagerness, he approached Thomas, their paths converging in the heart of the room.

"Thomas," Darcy began, his voice laced with a blend of vulnerability and longing, "I find myself entangled in a web of emotions, unsure of the path that lies before me. This connection I share with Charles has grown increasingly intimate, yet doubts and uncertainties plague me."

~

Thomas regarded Darcy with a compassionate gaze; his voice filled with understanding and empathy. "Love, my dear friend, is a complex labyrinth we must navigate. It is a journey that often defies societal expectations and challenges the very fabric of our being. But know that you are not alone in your struggles. As intricate as it may be, the heart seeks what it yearns for, and it is our duty to honor its desires."

Darcy's shoulders relaxed, a weight lifting from his chest as he absorbed Thomas's words. The warmth of friendship and guidance enveloped him, offering a glimmer of clarity amid his inner turmoil. "I thank you for your wisdom, Thomas," he said, his voice filled with gratitude. "To have a confidant such as you is a gift beyond measure."

With a shared understanding, Darcy and Thomas stood together in the dimly lit room, their hearts entwined in a bond of friendship that would guide them through the labyrinth of love. As the sun dipped lower in the sky and the colors of twilight enveloped the countryside, they embarked on a journey of self-discovery, their footsteps echoing through the halls of their shared existence.

DARCY TURNED to face his dear friend, grateful for the distraction from his own tumultuous emotions. Thomas was one of the few people who knew about Darcy's blossoming relationship with Bingley, and their bond had only grown stronger. There was a rare comfort in this shared secret, an intimacy that transcended mere friendship.

"Thomas," Darcy began hesitantly, "I have been struggling with my relationship with Bingley. I ... I need guidance."

A knowing smile played upon Thomas's lips as he closed the distance between them. "My dear friend," he murmured, placing a reassuring hand on Darcy's tense shoulder, "you know you can trust me with your deepest concerns."

Darcy looked into Thomas's eyes, feeling the weight of their emotional bond and their trust. He sensed a genuine desire to help in Thomas's gaze, a willingness to share his vulnerability.

"Thank you, Thomas," Darcy whispered, feeling the knot in

his chest unravel. "Your friendship means more to me than I could ever express."

"Come, let us retire to your study and discuss this further," Thomas suggested, leading the way with a gentle touch on Darcy's arm. "I have a feeling that together, we can find the clarity you seek."

❧

SEATED in the dimly lit study, Darcy hesitated before speaking, acutely aware of the gravity of what he was about to share. Thomas sat opposite him, a reassuring presence, his eyes soft and understanding. The fire crackled in the hearth, casting warm shadows across their faces.

"Thomas," Darcy began, his voice barely above a whisper, "you know how much I care for Bingley. But our love ... it requires such discretion."

"Of course," Thomas murmured, leaning in closer, his knee brushing against Darcy's. "We live in a society that does not accept love between men like us. It is a heavy burden, but one we must bear."

Darcy nodded, feeling the weight of his friend's words as they echoed his thoughts. He drew a shaky breath, then continued, his voice tinged with uncertainty. "I have encountered some... difficulties in our intimate moments. You see, sir, my size –" Darcy paused, swallowing hard, his cheeks flushed with embarrassment. "My cock, Thomas, measures twelve inches when fully erect."

Thomas's eyes widened slightly, but his expression remained compassionate. "That is quite... impressive, Darcy," he said gently. "But I can understand how it might present challenges in your lovemaking."

"Indeed," Darcy agreed, his hands trembling as he clasped them together. "I fear I lack the technical prowess necessary to pleasure Bingley properly. I do not wish to cause him pain, but I cannot deny the intensity of my desire for him."

"Your vulnerability speaks volumes of your devotion, Darcy," Thomas replied, grasping one of Darcy's hands. "It takes great courage to admit this, and I commend you for it."

DARCY LOOKED DOWN at their entwined fingers, the warmth of Thomas's touch providing a modicum of comfort amidst his turmoil. "I long to improve, Thomas," he confessed, his voice laced with desperation. "I wish to be the lover that Bingley deserves."

"Then let us work together to find a solution," Thomas suggested, his voice firm yet tender. "We can explore new techniques and methods to ensure your lovemaking is pleasurable and safe."

"Thank you, my friend," Darcy whispered, his eyes meeting Thomas again. "Your support means more to me than words could ever convey."

Darcy's heart raced as he watched the subtle change in Thomas's expression, a mix of surprise and intrigue. When Thomas coughed softly, Darcy could see the astonishment flicker in his eyes.

"TWELVE INCHES, YOU SAY?" Thomas inquired, his voice laced with an unmistakable tinge of curiosity, his eyes alight with intrigue.

Darcy, though hesitant, summoned the courage to respond, aware that the intimate knowledge he was about to reveal might elicit a range of reactions from his dear friend. "Yes," he replied, his voice tinged with uncertainty, "such is the extent of my...endowment. I do hope that is not a problem, dear friend."

Thomas, his gaze fixed upon Darcy with a renewed interest, murmured in a low, thoughtful tone. "Remarkable," he breathed, his words laden with admiration and comprehension. "One can certainly understand why you might face certain challenges with such a prodigious gift."

His cheeks tinged with a blush, Darcy found himself the subject of Thomas's scrutinizing stare. His vulnerability in that moment was palpable as he exposed his deepest insecurities to a trusted confidant. "Indeed," he conceded, his voice betraying his self-consciousness. "And it is precisely for this reason that I seek your guidance, Thomas."

LEANING BACK IN HIS CHAIR, Thomas assumed an air of contemplation, his countenance marked by a thoughtful expression. The weight of Darcy's request lingered in the air, demanding careful consideration. After a measured pause, Thomas seemed to arrive at a decision, a glimmer of resolve dancing in his eyes.

"Very well, my dear friend," Thomas declared, his voice resonating with a newfound sense of confidence and authority. "I shall undertake the role of your mentor, guiding you through a special tutorial session on the art of passionate intimacy. With my experience and expertise, I assure you that you shall become the lover Bingley rightly deserves."

Darcy's eyes shimmered with hope, the depth of his gratitude evident in his gaze. "Truly?" he whispered, his voice filled with awe and relief. "You would do this for me?"

A warm smile graced Thomas's lips, banishing any lingering doubts that may have clouded Darcy's mind. "Of course," he affirmed, his words carrying the weight of steadfast friendship. "For what purpose do we have dear friends if not to support and guide one another through life's most intimate journeys?"

As the dim light of the drawing room embraced them, Darcy

and Thomas forged a bond more vital than ever, bound by trust, friendship, and a shared commitment to navigating the intricacies of desire. With Thomas as his mentor, Darcy embarked upon a journey of self-discovery, armed with newfound knowledge and the unwavering support of a confidant who would lead him into the realm of unbridled passion.

A PROFOUND SENSE of relief washed over Darcy, his entire being trembling with anticipation as he fully comprehended the magnitude of Thomas's offer. With his friend's guidance, he would conquer his inner demons and insecurities and unlock the ability to bestow unparalleled pleasure upon his beloved Bingley. The weight of his anxieties began to dissipate, replaced by a newfound confidence that surged through his veins.

"Thank you, Thomas," Darcy murmured, his voice laden with emotion, his words a heartfelt expression of gratitude. "I cannot express the depth of my appreciation."

Embodying grace and generosity, Thomas dismissed Darcy's thanks with a wave, his noble countenance radiating a sense of purpose. Rising from his seat, he assumed the mentor role, ready to embark on this transformative journey. "Think nothing of it," he replied, his tone resonating with warmth and reassurance. "Now, my dear friend, let us prepare for the lesson ahead."

As THEY BEGAN to make their way toward the sanctuary of Darcy's private chambers, the air was thick with a mixture of trepidation and excitement. Darcy's mind buzzed with anticipation, a kaleidoscope of emotions swirling within him like a tempestuous storm. He knew all too well that the path he was about to tread would be fraught with challenges, but with Thomas at his side, he felt an unshakeable resolve. Together, they would conquer the unknown, exploring the depths of passion and pleasure that awaited them.

"Rest assured, Darcy," Thomas assured him, his hand gently resting upon Darcy's shoulder in a gesture of encouragement and support. "I shall unveil the secrets of ardor and ecstasy so you may share them with your beloved Bingley."

Darcy's heart swelled with gratitude, his trust in Thomas unwavering. "My body and every fiber of my being are in your good hands, kind sir," he declared, a touch of playful intensity imbuing his words. "Let us commence this journey, for we stand on the precipice of a new chapter in our lives."

With determination and desire coursing through their veins, Darcy and Thomas ventured into the realm of passion and sensuality, their souls intertwined in a dance of exploration and fulfillment. The stage was set, and the curtains were drawn as they embarked upon a voyage of pleasure and self-discovery that would forever alter the course of their lives.

SEX LESSONS

Darcy's heart pounded as he watched Bertram in the dimly lit chamber, the flickering candlelight casting golden shadows on the walls. Thomas stood before him, a picture of poised confidence, his eyes filled with an intensity that thrilled and unnerved Darcy. The air was heavy with anticipation, and the scent of beeswax mingled with the subtle aroma of their masculine musk.

"Are you ready?" Thomas asked, his voice low and inviting. He began to unbutton his waistcoat, fingers deftly moving over each fastening. As the garment fell open, it revealed the sculpted planes of his chest, a sight that stirred Darcy's desire further.

"Y-yes," Darcy stammered, captivated by the gradual unveiling of Thomas' body. Bertram continued, methodically removing each piece of clothing as if performing a tantalizing striptease. His breeches were the last to go, leaving him standing proudly in nothing but his linen drawers.

"Before we start," Thomas said, reaching for a small vial he had been carrying in his trousers pocket, "we'll need this." The liquid inside glistened in the candlelight, promising to ease their entry into this newfound world of pleasure.

"Of course," Darcy murmured, his gaze fixed on his friend's lithe form, the curve of his hips, and the swell of his thighs. Deeply, He felt a yearning that only Thomas could help him understand.

∾

"COME HERE, DARCY," Thomas beckoned, his voice gentle yet insistent. "Let me guide you."

The lessons commenced with Bertram instructing Darcy on preparing a lover for intimacy using his tongue and mouth. As they reclined on a plush chaise longue, Thomas gently encouraged Darcy to explore his backside's supple skin and taut muscles. Darcy hesitated at first, but Thomas's reassuring words and the warmth of his body urged him onward.

"Relax," Thomas murmured as Darcy tentatively caressed his ass with his lips, "and let your instincts guide you."

Darcy's confidence grew under Thomas's expert tutelage as the afternoon wore on. The two men experimented with various techniques and positions, each one bringing them closer to the brink of ecstasy. Their connection deepened with every touch, their bodies attuned to one another's needs and desires.

"Remember this, Darcy," Thomas gasped between passionate kisses, "the key is to be attentive and responsive to your lover's pleasure."

∾

"THOMAS," Darcy whispered, his voice trembling with a potent mixture of arousal and gratitude. "I cannot express my gratitude for opening my eyes to this clandestine world of passion and pleasure."

His breath is slightly ragged; Thomas meets Darcy's gaze

tenderly, his eyes reflecting a profound affection. "My dear friend," he replied, his voice laced with a hint of huskiness, "I only embarked upon this journey because I care deeply for you. I know the truth of your love for Bingley, and I want to aid you in your quest for fulfillment."

Their intimate connection continued to deepen, their bodies entwined in a dance of shared ecstasy. Each touch and caress spoke volumes of their unspoken desires as they immersed themselves in a haze of sensual exploration and mutual satisfaction. Time seemed to cease its relentless march as they surrendered to the powerful currents of desire that coursed through their veins.

As the evening shadows gathered, a sense of completion settled upon Darcy's being. The lessons he had absorbed from Thomas, the intimate secrets of passion and pleasure that had been unveiled to him, had ignited a newfound confidence. He was no longer burdened by self-doubt or insecurities, but he was ready to share this profound knowledge with his beloved Bingley.

With renewed purpose and self-assurance, Darcy's thoughts turned to the future, envisioning the intimate moments he and Bingley would share. Their love, once restrained by uncertainty, was now poised to flourish in all its splendor. As darkness enveloped the room, Darcy knew he was no longer the same man who had embarked upon this voyage with trepidation.

THE ROOM WAS FILLED with the sweet scent of arousal, and Darcy marveled at the intimate connection he shared with Thomas. Their bodies glistened with sweat, a testament to their passionate explorations. Darcy felt a surge of confidence as he began to understand the true depths of pleasure he could bring to another man.

"Thomas," Darcy murmured, his voice laced with desire, "I

want to try something new."

"Anything you wish, dear friend," Thomas replied, his eyes alight with curiosity and excitement. "I am here to guide you in discovering your desires and abilities."

"Then I want to experiment with different ways of thrusting so that I can learn how best to please my lover," Darcy declared, determination etched across his handsome features.

"Ah, the art of penetration," Thomas said with a knowing smile, "a skill that requires finesse and sensitivity. Come, let us explore this together."

Darcy positioned himself behind Thomas, who eagerly presented his ass. Darcy took a moment to appreciate the sight before him: Thomas's firm, round buttocks, slick with sweat and desire. He could see the delicate entrance to Thomas's body, inviting him to delve deeper.

"REMEMBER, MY DEAR DARCY," Thomas advised, his voice filled with guidance and longing, "it is of utmost importance to commence this intimate dance with a deliberate and unhurried tempo. Observe my every reaction, for in them lies the key to unlocking the pinnacle of pleasure."

Darcy, his heart hammering within his chest, absorbed Thomas's words with rapt attention, savoring the anticipation that coursed through his veins. With a steady hand and a tender resolve, he embarked upon the gradual insertion of his impressive length, inch by glorious inch, ensuring Thomas's comfort and readiness for the sensations yet to come.

"Good," Thomas moaned, his voice laced with a heady desire and encouragement. His body arched, a silent plea for Darcy to continue on this path of shared bliss. "Now, my dear friend, experiment with the tempo of your movements. Begin with gentle, shallow motions, teasing the depths of pleasure, before gradually building to deeper, more potent strokes."

Eager to please and learn, Darcy embraced Thomas's guidance, his every movement a testament to his dedication. With each carefully measured thrust, he reveled in the pleasure that escaped Thomas's lips, a melody that surged through the air, intoxicating their souls. Knowing he could bestow such ecstasy upon his partner fueled his desire, igniting a blazing fire.

"Listen, Darcy," Thomas panted, his grip on the sheets tightening as waves of pleasure coursed through him. "Attune yourself to my body's responses, the subtle nuances of my reactions. Allow them to guide you, shaping the path towards unparalleled pleasure."

Darcy's eyes never wavered, locked onto the point where their bodies joined as if he could discern the very essence of their connection. He absorbed the intricacies of their union, the raw intensity that fueled his every move. "I feel it, Thomas," he whispered, his voice a delicate murmur amidst the intensity of their passion. "I am attuned to your pleasure, and it intertwines with my own, creating a symphony that resonates within me."

A shuddering gasp escaped Thomas's lips, his body trembling with a potent cocktail of desire and need. "Splendid," he gasped, his voice filled with a hunger that matched Darcy's own. "Now, my dear friend, venture into angles and positions. Tilt your hips and shift your stance. With each subtle adjustment, you unlock new dimensions of sensation, embracing the uncharted territories of pleasure that await both you and your beloved."

Enveloped by a haze of desire and shared exploration, the boundaries of pleasure expanded with each shift, each change of position, as they delved deeper into the realm of unbridled ecstasy. Together, they navigated their shared desire as Darcy began to understand the power of his cock to pleasure other men.

DARCY FOLLOWED THOMAS'S ADVICE, and his efforts were rewarded with moans and sighs. As they continued to explore the myriad ways in which they could bring pleasure to one another, the room seemed to vibrate with their passion.

"Thomas," Darcy breathed, sweat beading on his brow, "your guidance has opened up a world of possibility for me."

"Then we have succeeded, my dear friend," Thomas replied, his voice husky with satisfaction. "Remember these lessons, and use them to bring happiness and fulfillment to your beloved Bingley."

As the last light of day faded outside their window, Darcy and Thomas lay entwined, sated and content. As Darcy closed his eyes, visions of future moments of passion with Bingley danced through his mind, filling him with a profound sense of hope and anticipation.

WITH THEIR BODIES slick with sweat and the air heavy with the scent of their passion, Darcy and Thomas indulged in a moment of respite. Their breaths mingled together as they lay entwined on the plush bedcovers, savoring the heat and connection between them.

"Your progress astounds me, Darcy," Thomas murmured, his fingertips tracing lazy circles on Darcy's chest. "But there is yet more to learn if you wish to unravel all the secrets of carnal pleasure."

A shiver of anticipation ran down Darcy's spine at Thomas's words. His desire, once a flickering flame, had grown into a roaring inferno under his friend's tutelage. "I am eager to continue, Thomas. Show me everything you know."

"Very well," Thomas replied, his eyes darkening with lust. He guided Darcy to a nearby chaise longue and settled himself upon it; his legs spread invitingly. "Let us explore more advanced techniques."

Throughout the evening, Darcy and Thomas experimented with varying depths and rhythms, finding joy in the push and pull of their intimate dance. As the hours passed, their coupling grew more intense, their connection deepening with each touch, each shared breath, and each cry of pleasure.

"Thomas," Darcy panted during one particularly heated exchange, "your friendship means more to me than you can ever know. I trust you completely."

"Your trust honors me, Darcy," Thomas replied, his voice raw with emotion. "I swear on my life that your secrets are safe."

DARCY AND THOMAS engaged in several more fucking sessions; each break was spent catching their breath and exploring one another's bodies with tender curiosity. They kissed deeply, tongues dancing together, as their hands roamed freely over muscles and sinew.

"Notice how my body responds to your touch, Darcy," Thomas encouraged, his breath hitching as Darcy's fingers traced the curve of his hip. "See how it arches towards you, begging for more."

"Your desire is a heady aphrodisiac, Thomas," Darcy whispered back, his fingers slipping lower, teasing the sensitive skin just beneath the waistband of Thomas's underwear. "It makes me feel powerful, capable of bringing you to ecstasy."

"Indeed," Thomas sighed, his eyes fluttering shut at the exquisite sensation. "And in turn, your newfound confidence has made you irresistible."

Darcy and Thomas finally collapsed into each other's arms, their bodies spent, their souls fulfilled. They were two men bound together by shared secrets, passion, and trust, and their connection had grown stronger.

MISS BINGLEY TO THE RESCUE

The evening sun cast a warm glow over Darcy's study at Pember-
ley, the golden light highlighting the intricate details of the wood
paneling and the fine bindings on his extensive collection of books.
Fitzwilliam Darcy stood by the window, his tall, muscular frame
silhouetted against the fading sun. His dark eyes gazed out over
the sprawling estate, but it was not the view that held his atten-
tion — it was the man standing behind him.

Charles Bingley, his blond curls pulled back in an effortless ponytail, moved closer to Darcy, his smaller yet equally powerful frame pressing against the taller man. The scent of Bingley's cologne filled Darcy's nostrils, intoxicating him with its rich, earthy aroma. As their bodies met, their electricity crackled like a fire in the hearth.

"Charles," Darcy whispered, feeling the heat of Bingley's breath on his neck as the other man's hands slid under his fine waistcoat, fingers dancing along the lines of his well-toned chest.

"Fitzy," Bingley murmured, nipping at Darcy's earlobe as he explored the other man's body, their hearts pounding in unison.

They moved together, a passionate dance of desire fueled by longing and need.

~

As Darcy turned to face Bingley, their lips met in a searing kiss that threatened to consume them both. Hands roamed along sculpted muscles and taut skin beneath. Darcy marveled at the sight before him, the way the dying sunlight played upon Bingley's golden curls and danced across his smooth, pale skin.

"God, you are so wonderful, my love. I have never met a man as masculine as you," Darcy breathed, capturing Bingley's mouth once more as they embraced, their entwined limbs creating a tangle of desire.

Their passions rose to a fever pitch, the two men exploring each other's bodies with an urgency that spoke of their deep connection. Every touch, every taste, every whispered endearment only served to heighten the pleasure they found in one another's arms.

As Darcy and Bingley lay entwined on the study floor, lost in ecstasy, neither noticed the door silently opening behind them. The tension in the room shifted abruptly as Caroline Bingley stood in the doorway, her eyes widening in shock at the sight before her.

"Charles!" she gasped, her voice a mixture of disbelief and horror. "What on earth...?"

The sense of urgency between Darcy and Bingley was suddenly replaced by panic as they scrambled to separate from one another, hastily attempting to regain some semblance of decorum. Their eyes darted between each other and Caroline, who stood rooted to the spot, her face pale and her hands trembling at her sides.

~

DARCY, ever the master of composure, swiftly pulled away from Bingley and adjusted his cravat with a deft flick of his wrist. His dark eyes locked onto Caroline's as he attempted to disarm the situation with the charm that had beguiled countless hearts.

"Miss Bingley," he began, his voice smooth and steady despite the thundering of his heart. "Your arrival is, as always, most unexpected."

Bingley quickly recovered, his innate wit shining through as he straightened his attire. "Caroline," he said lightly, a faint smile playing on his lips, "you have a talent for impeccable timing."

Caroline blinked rapidly, her shock giving way to disbelief as she surveyed the scene before her: Darcy, flushed and disheveled, still exuding an air of magnetism that seemed only to intensify the room's charged atmosphere; and her brother Charles, his golden curls tousled and his blue eyes alight with a fire she had never before seen.

"Ch-Charles," she stammered, her face paling further as she struggled to comprehend the depths of their indiscretion. "I ... I do not ..."

"Perhaps," Darcy interjected gently, his eyes never leaving hers, "it would be best if Mr. Bingley were to step out for a moment so that we might discuss this matter privately?"

"Of course," Bingley acquiesced, casting one last lingering glance at Darcy before slipping silently from the room.

"PLEASE, MISS BINGLEY, SIT DOWN." Darcy gestured towards a pair of plush armchairs near the fireplace, the warmth emanating from the crackling flames doing little to alleviate the chill that now permeated the study. "Allow me to order some tea for our discussion."

Moments later, they found themselves seated opposite one another, the steaming cups of tea providing a small measure of comfort amidst the storm of emotions that threatened to overwhelm them. Darcy observed Caroline's delicate hands trembling as she clutched her teacup, her eyes staring unseeingly into the swirling liquid.

"Caroline," he began softly, well aware of the weight his words carried in this delicate situation, "I understand that what you have witnessed is both shocking and difficult to comprehend." He paused, allowing the gravity of his admission to hang in the air. "But know that whatever you may think of me, or your brother, our feelings for one another are genuine and true."

Caroline's gaze flicked upwards, meeting his with an intensity that belied her vulnerability. "Fitzwilliam," she whispered, her voice barely audible above the crackling fire. "How... how long has this been going on?"

"Long enough," Darcy replied, his expression a mixture of sadness and resolve. "Long enough for us to know that we cannot deny the truth of our desires any longer."

DARCY'S EYES locked onto Caroline's, an unwavering calmness in his gaze as he prepared to address her concerns. Amidst the flickering shadows cast by the dancing flames of the fireplace, the tension between them became palpable.

"Caroline," Darcy began, his voice steady and soothing, "it is crucial for a family such as ours to support and accept one another, especially in times of uncertainty." He paused, studying her reaction. Her ice-blue eyes reflected the firelight, shimmering with unshed tears.

"You must know that your brother, Charles, has always been there for you, providing you with love, guidance, and even financial support when necessary." Darcy leaned forward, his muscular chest straining against the delicate fabric of his shirt as he continued. "Now, more than ever, he needs your understanding and compassion."

Caroline lowered her gaze, her long lashes casting dark crescents onto her porcelain cheeks. She took a deep breath, her slender fingers curling around the delicate handle of the teacup. "I know, Fitzwilliam... I know that Charles loves me dearly, and I do not wish to cause him pain."

"Then it is time for you to return that love and support," Darcy urged gently, his dark curls framing his handsome face, the passionate intensity in his eyes never wavering. "He deserves nothing less from you, Caroline."

SILENCE ENVELOPED THE ROOM, punctuated only by the grandfather clock's ticking and the fire's soft crackle. The scent of Earl Grey tea wafted through the air, mingling with the heavy musk of their previous encounter. Time seemed to slow as they both contemplated the gravity of the situation.

Darcy's mind drifted back to the heated moments he had shared with Bingley just minutes before—their bodies entwined, the taste of each other's lips lingering, the feel of Bingley's strong hands on his skin. He yearned to be close to him again, their desires finally free to entangle them in each other's embrace.

Caroline's voice interrupted his thoughts. "You are fair, and you are right, Fitzwilliam. I must do better for my brother." She looked up at him, her eyes now resolute with determination. "I will find a way to support Charles and accept his choices, no matter how unexpected. He is my brother, after all; therefore, you, Mr. Darcy, have also become a brother to me, yes?"

Darcy nodded, a small, relieved smile tugging at the corners of his lips. The muscles in his broad shoulders relaxed slightly as he leaned back into his chair, allowing himself to bask in the warmth of Caroline's newfound understanding.

"THANK YOU, CAROLINE," he murmured, his voice laden with gratitude. "Your willingness to embrace change and support your brother will not go unnoticed. I assure you, we are both deeply grateful."

In return, Caroline offered a hesitant smile, acknowledging the unspoken bond forged between them in this moment of vulnerability and acceptance. They sat in silence, sipping their tea and contemplating the road ahead – a path lined with challenges and uncertainties but also love and understanding.

Caroline's delicate brows furrowed, her eyes filling with tears as she looked away from Darcy. She clenched her hands into fists, her knuckles turning white as she struggled to understand the weight of his words. "But it will never be simple, will it, Fitzwilliam," she whispered, her voice wavering. "You know how society judges those who do not conform to its expectations."

Darcy leaned forward, his gaze softening with empathy as he reached out and gently took Caroline's hand. "I do understand, dear Caroline," he said. His strong fingers traced delicate patterns on her skin, the touch comforting and charged with unspoken need. "But I also know what it means to deny one's true desires, to suppress the essence of who we are."

He paused for a moment, collecting his thoughts. "When I first realized my attraction to men, I felt shame, fear, and loneliness. But over time, I learned to embrace my true self, to accept that love can take many forms." Darcy's eyes met Caroline's, his gaze unwavering. "Would you truly want another woman to be married to a man who cannot love her completely? Can you imagine yourself in such a marriage, Caroline?"

CAROLINE'S BREATH caught in her throat as the truth of Darcy's words struck her. She had never considered that perspective, too focused on the potential scandal and the harm it could cause to their family's reputation. As her mind reeled, she envisioned herself trapped in a loveless, passionless marriage, shackled by convention and obligation.

"Of course not, Fitzwilliam," she admitted, her voice barely audible as she choked back a sob. "I would never wish that upon myself or any other woman."

"Then you must consider Charles's happiness as well," Darcy urged, his voice firm yet gentle. "He deserves the same opportunity for love and fulfillment that you do."

Caroline's heart ached as she took in Darcy's words, her defenses slowly crumbling under the weight of empathy and understanding. She felt exposed, vulnerable, and liberated in a way she had not experienced before.

"Very well," she whispered, her voice trembling with emotion. "I will strive to accept and support Charles and his choices more. I owe him that much."

"Thank you, Caroline," Darcy said softly, reassuringly squeezing her hand. His eyes conveyed a deep gratitude, and Caroline felt a newfound connection blossoming between them —a bond forged through vulnerability and truth.

AS THEY SAT TOGETHER in quiet contemplation, Darcy's thoughts again drifted to Bingley. He longed for the warmth of their touch, the taste of their mouths melding together in fierce passion. A shiver ran down his spine as he recalled the feeling of Bingley's strong hands gripping his thighs, their desires entwined like serpents in the heat of their fervor.

And now, with Caroline's begrudging acceptance, perhaps they could finally explore the depths of their love without fear, embarking on a journey of discovery and fulfillment that would transcend the boundaries of society's expectations.

Caroline's eyes glistened with unshed tears, her chest heaving as Darcy's words pierced through the armor she had built around herself. Her heart raced, a storm of conflicting emotions threatening to overwhelm her.

"Caroline," Darcy began gently, his voice filled with empathy and understanding. "I know this is difficult for you, but I need you to consider how your actions have affected Charles."

Her breath hitched in her throat, and she looked away, unable to meet his gaze any longer. She recalled the countless times she had tried to direct her brother's attention towards more socially acceptable suitors, all while knowing full well that his heart belonged elsewhere.

"HAVE I BEEN SO BLIND?" she whispered, anguish coloring her words.

"Oh, dearest, Caroline. None of us are truly without fault," Darcy replied softly, reassuringly touching her shoulder. "But it is never too late for us to change, to grow."

With a choked sob, she finally allowed her defenses to crumble, her body wracked by the force of her emotions. The dam that had held back her tears broke, and they streamed down her cheeks, staining the fine silk of her gown.

"Charles!" she cried out as if he were in the room, her voice hoarse with regret. "I am so sorry, my dear brother."

Darcy watched her with sympathy and relief, relieved she was finally accepting the truth. He let her weep, knowing these tears were necessary for her acceptance and growth.

"Caroline," he said quietly once her sobs had subsided. "Promise me, from now on, that you will be a better sister, friend, and ally to Charles."

SHE NODDED FERVENTLY, wiping away her tears with trembling hands. "I promise, Darcy. I will do everything I can to support him in pursuing happiness, even if it means going against society's expectations."

"Thank you," Darcy replied, his voice filled with gratitude. "That is all any of us can ask for."

As their conversation drew to a close, Caroline could not help but steal glances at Darcy, taking in the strong lines of his jaw and the broad expanse of his chest beneath his fine waistcoat. Despite her recent emotional turmoil, she could not deny the allure she found in him—a man who could arouse desire and wield words like a skilled surgeon, cutting through her defenses and revealing her innermost vulnerabilities.

"Your love for Mr. Charles is sincere and beautiful, Mr. Darcy," she said quietly, her voice still shaky from her earlier breakdown. "I can see now why he holds you in such high regard."

Darcy, touched by her words, offered her a small, warm smile. "And I am grateful for your understanding, Miss Bingley. It means more than you know to both of us."

Their newfound bond forged in vulnerability and acceptance, they sat together in companionable silence, each contemplating the challenges and triumphs ahead for their unconventional family. In the shadows of Pemberley's study, they found solace and strength within one another, ready to embrace a future of love and understanding, no matter their obstacles.

A FLEETING MOMENT passed before Darcy extended his arms towards Caroline, who hesitated for a heartbeat before leaning into the embrace. As they held each other, their tears melded together on cheeks flushed with vulnerability and forgiveness. The weight of their shared understanding hung in the air, as tangible as the antique tomes that lined the walls of Pemberley's study.

"Caroline," Darcy whispered, his voice thick with emotion.

"Your strength in facing this revelation is admirable. Remember that we are all human and capable of change."

Caroline nodded against his chest, finding solace in the warmth of his embrace and the steady rhythm of his heart. She breathed deeply, taking in the rich, masculine scent that clung to him like a second skin. She wondered if her brother had experienced the same intoxicating sensation during their earlier encounter.

"Thank you, Mr. Darcy," she replied, her words muffled by the fabric of his waistcoat. "I promise I will do my best to support Charles and be there for him."

As they pulled away from one another, their eyes met, and in that lingering gaze, they silently acknowledged the profound connection they now shared. It was as if a veil had been lifted, exposing them to the raw truths of life and love previously obscured by societal constraints.

"LET us now move forward with this newfound understanding," Darcy said gently, his hand lingering on Caroline's arm as they separated. "Together, we can help Charles navigate these uncharted waters."

"Agreed," Caroline replied, her voice firm yet imbued with a softness that spoke of a woman transformed. "I am grateful for your guidance, Mr. Darcy. Together, we shall be a force to be reckoned with. You will now be like a brother to me. And that makes me deliriously happy."

As the door to the study closed behind them, the dimly lit room bore silent witness to the beginning of a new chapter in the lives of Fitzwilliam Darcy, Charles Bingley, and Caroline Bingley. United by an unbreakable bond forged in the crucible of truth, they would face the challenges ahead with courage, understanding, and unwavering support.

The future held no guarantees, but as they walked down the

halls of Pemberley, their shoulders squared against adversity, it was clear that they were prepared to defy convention and embrace the beauty of love in all its forms. And perhaps, just perhaps, they would discover that the path less traveled could lead to the most exhilarating of destinations.

YOUR WISH IS MY COMMAND, MR. BINGLEY

In its descent towards the horizon, the sun painted the grand drawing-room of Pemberley with a warm, golden hue. Fitzwilliam Darcy, a figure of strength and grace, stood near the crackling fireplace, his commanding presence heightened by the play of light and shadow. His heart stirred with a potent longing as his gaze fixated on Charles Bingley, who was engrossed in animated conversation with Caroline.

Darcy's eyes traced the elegant curve of Bingley's neck, the delicate vulnerability it possessed as he tilted his head back in laughter. The tousled curls that adorned his head seemed to beckon Darcy, teasing him with their playful allure. A shiver of desire danced along Darcy's spine, and he found himself stealing clandestine glances at Bingley's firm thighs, encased in tight breeches that left little to the imagination.

"Shall we retire for the evening, dear Bingley?" Darcy suggested his voice a low, husky murmur laden with unspoken desire. "The day has been eventful, and a restful reprieve may be just what we need."

Bingley's cerulean eyes, brimming with a shared under-standing, locked with Darcy's gaze. Their unspoken promises hung heavily in the air, a silent conversation that spoke volumes. Their connection was palpable, an invisible thread that bound them together, drawing them inexorably closer.

"Indeed," Bingley agreed, his voice a gentle affirmation of their mutual yearning. "I find myself weary, and the prospect of rest is most welcome."

The anticipation swelled within Darcy's chest, his heart pounding with trepidation and excitement. The time had come to embark on a journey of intimacy and discovery, a path that would forever alter the course of their lives. As they made their way toward the sanctuary of their chambers, Darcy's mind buzzed with anticipation, his thoughts consumed by the promise of shared passion and fulfillment.

CAROLINE NODDED, her newfound understanding evident in her compassionate smile. "I will ask your good Mr. Humphries to call for my carriage. I look forward to seeing you both tomorrow. Sleep well, gentlemen." With a swish of her skirts, she left the room, leaving Darcy and Bingley to navigate the simmering tension between them.

As the door closed behind her, Darcy stepped closer to Bing-ley, his hand brushing against the smaller man's cheek. "Charles," he murmured, his breath hot and urgent against Bing-ley's skin, "I cannot resist any longer."

"Nor can I, Fitzwilliam," Bingley whispered, his fingers tracing the outline of Darcy's strong jaw, trembling with anticipa-tion. "Take me to your bedchamber."

Their lips met in a searing kiss, tongues dancing together in a sensual tango of passion and desire. Darcy's hands roamed Bingley's body, gripping his waist and pulling him closer as if to meld their bodies into one.

"Please, Fitzwilliam," Bingley gasped between kisses, his chest heaving with the intensity of his need. "Take me now."

~

DARCY SCOOPED BINGLEY into his arms, carrying him towards the bedchamber with an urgency that matched the pounding of their hearts. Their eyes never left each other's, a silent vow passing between them in this moment of vulnerability, two souls laid bare before one another.

As they entered the dimly lit sanctuary, Darcy lowered Bingley onto the plush bed, their gazes locked in a heated exchange of lustful intent. Darcy's fingers worked feverishly at the buttons of Bingley's shirt, revealing the sculpted planes of his chest and abdomen, pale skin flushed with arousal.

"God, you are irresistible. I find you handsome and alluring," Darcy moaned, his voice thick with desire as he saw Bingley's body, clad only in tight, white undergarments that clung to every curve and contour. He could not resist the urge to explore the smaller man's frame, running reverent fingertips along the dips and ridges of muscle.

"Touch me, Fitzwilliam," Bingley urged, arching his back to meet Darcy's wandering hands, desperate for more contact. "I need to feel your hands on me."

"Your wish is my command," Darcy murmured, his breath hot against Bingley's earlobe as he tugged it gently with his teeth. His hands slid down Bingley's body, teasing the waistband of his undergarment before slipping beneath the fabric.

~

BINGLEY'S GASP filled the room as Darcy's skilled fingers began to work their magic, stroking and caressing in a rhythm that left both men breathless and aching for more.

"Please, Fitzwilliam," Bingley begged, his voice hoarse with need. "I cannot wait any longer."

"Neither can I, my love." And with that, they succumbed to their desires, their bodies entwined in a dance as old as time itself, their passion igniting the air around them. Together, they explored the depths of their love and lust, their vulnerability and connection allowing them to transcend the boundaries of propriety and convention. In this stolen moment, they were free to be their authentic selves—unapologetically, unreservedly, and unequivocally in love.

A FIRE CRACKLED SOFTLY in the dimly lit bed chamber, casting flickering shadows on the walls. The scent of the male musk of both men intensified the heady atmosphere. Darcy reclined in his plush armchair, his muscular legs stretched out before him, while Bingley knelt at his feet, his delicate hands massaging Darcy's calves through the fine fabric of his trousers.

"Your touch never ceases to amaze me, Charles," Darcy murmured, his eyes half-lidded as he gazed down at his lover with a mixture of desire and admiration.

"Nor does your beauty, Fitzwilliam," Bingley replied, lifting one of Darcy's legs onto his lap, allowing his fingers to explore the contours of the strong muscles hidden beneath the cloth. "You are a living work of art."

Darcy chuckled, the sound low and rich. "I could say the same of you, my love." He leaned forward, capturing Bingley's lips in a searing kiss, their tongues dancing together in a practiced rhythm.

As they parted, their breaths mingled, and Bingley returned his attention to Darcy's legs. His fingers deftly unfastened the buttons of Darcy's trousers, freeing the man's gigantic and swollen arousal from its constraints.

"Goodness, Fitzwilliam," Bingley whispered, his voice heavy with awe as his hand closed around Darcy's impressive length. "Truly, you possess a gift beyond compare."

Darcy nodded in agreement, his senses ablaze with desire, his eyes never leaving the sight of Bingley's skilled touch. The caress was slow, deliberate, teasing, and Darcy reveled in the exquisite sensation as Bingley's hand moved with practiced precision.

"Indeed, my dear Bingley," he murmured, his voice laced with appreciation. "Fortune smiles upon me, for I have found not only a willing partner but one who possesses an extraordinary talent."

A wicked grin curved Bingley's lips as he lowered his head, his breath warm against Darcy's throbbing flesh. "Shall I demonstrate the extent of my skill, Fitzwilliam?" he inquired, his voice a tantalizing promise.

Darcy's anticipation grew, his voice tight with longing as he replied, "By all means, Charles. Allow me to witness the depth of your expertise."

With that invitation, Bingley embarked on a journey of pleasure, his lips and tongue working in perfect harmony. He began teasingly swirling around the sensitive tip, his mouth enveloping Darcy's length with practiced finesse. Darcy's hands instinctively found their way into Bingley's golden curls, gripping them with desperation and arousal. Bingley's mastery of his art elicited a symphony of moans and whispered pleas from Darcy, each sound a testament to the waves of pleasure that coursed through his being.

"Charles... It would be best if you relented," Darcy warned, his voice strained with urgency. His breaths came in short gasps, his body teetering on the precipice of ecstasy. "I cannot withstand this exquisite torment much longer."

Bingley pulled away, a wicked glint dancing in his eyes. "Then let us elevate this moment to the pinnacle of remembrance," he suggested, his voice laced with a mischievous edge.

Darcy, his senses ablaze and his body aflame with desire met Bingley's gaze with a mixture of anticipation and trust. In that moment, he surrendered himself to the passion that bound them, ready to embrace the unknown and revel in the extraordinary. Together, they would craft a memory that would forever be etched in the tapestry of their shared desires.

HE STOOD BEFORE DARCY, his trembling fingers deftly unbuttoning the fabric of his trousers, allowing them to cascade down in a soft pool at his feet. The anticipation in the air was palpable, a tangible force that made Darcy's pulse quicken even further. His gaze, drawn inexorably to the sight before him, was met with the proud and resolute form of Bingley's arousal, standing tall and eager. It was a sight that stirred Darcy's deepest desires, rendering him breathless with need.

"Come here," Darcy commanded, his voice a low, husky murmur laden with desire, as he extended his hands towards Bingley, beckoning him closer. As Bingley obeyed, the air crackled with electricity, straddling Darcy's lap gracefully. Their bodies melded together, pressed skin to skin, as their lips collided once more in a fervent kiss that set their senses ablaze. The heat of their entwined flesh sent shivers down their spines, a testament to the fiery passion that coursed through their veins.

In their desperate quest for release, they rocked together, their bodies moving in unison, a symphony of desire. Each movement was a whisper of longing and a plea for fulfillment as their souls sought solace in the embrace of the other. The world around them faded insignificantly as they surrendered to the intoxicating rhythm of their shared desire.

~

"PLEASE, PLEASE, FITZWILLIAM," Bingley pleaded, his voice a gentle entreaty that hung delicately in the air, almost drowned out by the crackling of the fire. "Let us become one, bound together in this moment of transcendence. Pummel me with your engorged manhood. Plow me long and hard, good sir."

Darcy, his breaths ragged and strained, his heart pounding with urgency and tenderness, met Bingley's gaze with a deep understanding. With a reverence that matched his longing, he nodded, giving his consent to this sacred union. Their bodies, drenched in the warmth of their shared passion, moved as if guided by an unseen force, drawing them closer to the precipice of ecstasy.

As they merged, their souls intertwined in a dance of vulnerability and trust; they became one, transcending the boundaries of society and embracing the true essence of their desires. As their bodies moved in perfect harmony in that intimate space, they found a profound connection that surpassed the physical realm. It was a moment of sublime union, where pleasure and love intertwined, forging a bond that would endure beyond the confines of time.

With his newfound techniques, the sexual union between the two men was profound. Charles was ecstatic to have the man's enormous cock fully inserted up his ass. He felt he was finally at home with the man he loved. The more he encouraged Darcy, the better the pummeling fulfilled him. Pumping and pumping. The two men were in heaven together but firmly located on earth.

And in the hallowed silence of their shared sanctuary, their shared whispers of ecstasy mingled with the crackling of the fire, creating a symphony of pleasure that echoed through the chambers of their souls.

AND SO THEY both achieved an intense sexual orgasm, their bodies joining together in a union as old as time itself, their ecstasy cries echoing through Pemberley's hallowed halls. As they reached their peak, their love and passion for one another became an undeniable, unbreakable bond that would withstand the test of time and society's cruel judgments.

"Charles," Darcy breathed, his fingers tangled in Bingley's hair as they clung to one another, spent and sated. "My love for you knows no bounds."

"Nor does mine for you, Fitzwilliam," Bingley replied, tenderly kissing Darcy's sweat-slicked brow. "Together, we shall face whatever the world may throw at us."

"Indeed," Darcy agreed, pulling Bingley closer, their hearts beating as one in the stillness of the night. "Together, we are unstoppable."

"OH, THE SWEET ANTICIPATION, CHARLES," Darcy murmured, his voice filled with a heady mix of desire and longing. "I beseech you; show me the heights of pleasure we can ascend to as we dance this intimate dance together."

Bingley, his eyes alight with a flame of passion, met Darcy's gaze with equal fervor. A flush of anticipation rose in his cheeks as he leaned closer, his lips hovering tantalizingly close to Darcy's ear. "Fear not, my dear Fitzwilliam," he whispered, his voice a seductive melody that sent shivers down Darcy's spine. "I shall guide you to the pinnacle of ecstasy, where pleasure knows no bounds."

Darcy's breath hitched, his body responding eagerly to Bingley's promises. His hands trembled with anticipation and need as they sought Bingley's touch, yearning for the connection to ignite their shared passion. The air crackled with an electric charge, heavy with unspoken desires and whispered entreaties.

As Bingley's lips descended upon Darcy's, their mouths melded in a fervent kiss, a fusion of desire and hunger. Their tongues danced in an intricate rhythm, exploring the depths of each other's mouths with an intoxicating fervor. They became lost in a world of sensation, where time ceased to exist, and pleasure reigned supreme.

DARCY'S HANDS traced a path of fire along Bingley's sculpted torso, his fingertips memorizing the contours and dips of his lover's body. The fabric that separated them became an obstacle, and with a feverish urgency, they shed their garments, casting them aside as if to liberate their desires. Skin met skin, a symphony of warmth and connection that fueled their passion.

As they entwined upon the silken sheets, their bodies moved in perfect harmony, each touch and caress an expression of their shared longing. Bingley's hands, skilled and attentive, traversed the expanse of Darcy's body, leaving a trail of searing pleasure in their wake. They explored every inch, stoking the flames of desire until Darcy's senses were ablaze with an all-consuming need.

Their movements quickened, a crescendo of desire building within them. Sweat glistened upon their skin, a testament to the intensity of their union. The room filled with the symphony of their moans and gasps, a harmonious melody that echoed through the hallowed halls of passion.

Their bodies coiled together in the throes of ecstasy, breaths mingling as they reached the zenith of pleasure. Time stood still as they clung to one another, their hearts pounding in unison. Darcy and Bingley were no longer two separate souls but a single entity, bound by a love that defied societal conventions and embraced the true essence of their being.

As two lovers descended from the heights of bliss, their bodies entangled and sated, a profound sense of contentment settled upon them. Their gazes met, filled with a tenderness born from shared vulnerability and profound connection. In that intimate space, they found solace and completion, knowing that their union was a testament to the power of love and the beauty of embracing one's true desires.

DISCLAIMER

Within the pages of this book of gay erotica, a realm of fiction unfolds, delving into explicit territory meant for mature and consenting audiences. These stories, crafted by the imaginative hand of Griff Holland, a fictional character brought to life for your entertainment, beckon you to explore a world where passion and desire between same-sex partners take center stage.

It is crucial to recognize that these tales exist solely within the realm of fantasy and imagination. They do not depict the experiences or perspectives of any real-life individuals and should not be misconstrued as such. The author firmly disapproves of and does not endorse non-consensual or abusive behavior.

By embarking on this literary journey, the reader affirms that they are of legal age to engage with such content in accordance with their jurisdiction's laws. Furthermore, the reader acknowledges that they have willingly made the choice to delve into these stories. The author relinquishes any responsibility for the consequences that may arise from the readers' actions in response to the contents of this work. Therefore, if you are ready to embark on a voyage that blurs the lines between desire and fiction, step into this enchanting world with open eyes. The stories contained within will transport you to realms where passion reigns, boundaries expand, and consent serves as the guiding principle.

This book is dedicated to all the dreamers out there who, like myself, spent their youth wandering the streets of Boston in their imaginations, captivated by crime detection. We yearned for a place where we could rest our weary legs on the back of cop cars, where we could seek out partners amidst the hallowed halls of police locker rooms, and where we could find a male character who would ignite passionate nights within the corridors of stakeouts in abandoned warehouses. Ah, the irresistible allure of the charismatic Detective Lance Fortunato and the world he inhabits, which has captured our hearts and fired our imaginations.

To my dear readers, I extend my heartfelt gratitude for allowing me to accompany you on this thrilling journey as an author. I still remember my own youthful days, a mere high school student at the tender age of 18, when I too yearned for my very own Detective Fortunato to sweep me off my feet and join me in the exhilarating adventures life had in store. The memories of those times, filled with hope and dreams, hold a special place in my heart.

With the utmost gratitude and respect, I present this work to you. It is a humble offering, a tale woven with passion and love, inspired by a vision of a world where love knows no boundaries and where the captivating atmosphere of police precincts serves as a backdrop for our most cherished desires.

May this book serve as a conduit, transporting you to a realm where dreams come alive, where love reigns supreme, and where the essence of intense gay passion between men takes center stage.

With deep gratitude and respect,
Griff Holland

ABOUT THE AUTHOR

Griff Holland is a remarkable individual who defies the notion of an ordinary author. By day, he showcases his exceptional skills as a master architect, renowned for his expertise in preserving and revitalizing New England's historic treasures. With an artist's touch, he breathes new life into cherished landmarks, leaving a lasting impact on the architectural world. However, Griff's talents extend far beyond his architectural prowess.

In his earlier days, Griff was an Olympic skier, an adventurer who reveled in the thrill of pushing himself to the limits. The snow-covered peaks became his playground, and the adrenaline rush left an indelible mark on his soul. It is this exhilaration that spills onto the pages of his male erotica fiction, infusing his stories with a sense of passion and excitement.

When Griff is not immersed in the world of architectural restoration or embracing the thrill of alpine adventures, he seeks solace and purpose at his writing desk. Within the sanctuary of his imagination, he weaves intricate tales of male desire that transcend the ordinary. His plots are captivating, and his characters are complex, ensnaring readers from the very first sentence until the final page.

Yet, Griff's talents do not stop there. He is also a sought-after public speaker, frequently gracing television screens as an expert on home repair. He shares his knowledge and expertise with a warmth and approachability that endears him to all who encounter him, inspiring and motivating others along the way. His enthusiasm is contagious, making him a cherished figure in the literary world.

In the precious moments of free time, he cherishes, Griff embarks on outdoor escapades with his beloved canine companions. A devoted dog lover, he finds solace in nature's embrace, which rejuvenates his spirit and fuels his creativity.

Despite the accolades he has received, Griff remains remarkably humble and grounded. He is an eternal student of his craft, constantly seeking improvement and growth. Whether conquering snow-capped peaks or putting pen to paper, he approaches each endeavor with unwavering determination and an unwavering commitment to excellence.

Thus, the enigmatic and multifaceted Griff Holland continues to leave an indelible mark on the world. He is an artist of architecture, an adventurer of the slopes, a captivating author of desire, and a beacon of inspiration for all those who yearn to embrace their passions and forge their own paths.

ACKNOWLEDGMENTS

First and foremost, the author extends heartfelt gratitude to the dedicated gay erotica enthusiasts whose passion and enthusiasm form the foundation of the stories in this collection. It is important to note that these tales are presented as works of fiction, aiming to celebrate the wide range of human desire and sensuality that knows no boundaries. The men within these pages are courageous and unapologetically themselves, finding strength in embracing their sexuality and sensuality. They forge connections and camaraderie with fellow individuals who appreciate thoughtfully crafted erotica. It is the daring spirits of these readers, the kinksters, who inspire and breathe life into these stories, allowing them to unfold and thrive.

The author expresses deep gratitude to their beloved partner, Mitchell, whose unwavering support has been invaluable. Mitchell's love and encouragement have been the guiding light that led the author to bring this book to fruition. In the quiet moments at home, their presence is enchanting. Mitchell's constant inspiration extends even to the gym, where they make the author feel like the best version of themselves. The author is grateful for the solid foundation Mitchell has provided for this creative journey.

Appreciation is sincerely extended to the editor and beta readers for their invaluable feedback and guidance. Their keen insights and thoughtful suggestions have shaped the story into its final form. Their unwavering commitment to excellence has been instrumental in the creation of this work. The author deeply cherishes their attention to detail and dedication to refining the story.

A special tribute is dedicated to the LGBTQ+ community, whose tireless advocacy and unwavering fight for equality and acceptance have paved the way for stories like this to be told and embraced. The community's resilience in the face of adversity serves as a beacon of hope and inspiration. The author stands in awe of their continued activism, which has brought about significant change throughout history.

The author extends heartfelt gratitude to the dear readers for embarking on this journey together. They sincerely hope that this collection of stories has brought joy, pleasure, and a deeper appreciation for the complexities of love, desire, and human connection. The readers' support has been the driving force behind the author's creativity, and their willingness to explore this world alongside them fills their heart with profound gratitude.

May these tales of passion and romance continue to resonate in the readers' hearts, celebrating the beauty of love in all its forms. The author thanks each and every reader for being an integral part of this creative adventure. They hope that the power of storytelling will inspire and unite everyone who encounters these pages.

READERS—GOT IDEAS?

Griff Holland, an author whose talents shine in the realm of erotica, finds himself entangled in an intriguing predicament. The abundance of creativity from his devoted readers is both a blessing and a challenge. Their ceaseless stream of story ideas is a testament to his magnetic storytelling, but it also takes its toll on his muse, leaving her in dire need of respite.

As the morning sun casts its gentle glow upon his writing chamber, Griff opens his email inbox to discover a veritable flood of tantalizing story ideas from his ardent admirers. With eager anticipation, he delves into each missive, immersing himself in the sea of imagination that lies before him. The outpouring of passion and ingenuity within those emails is nothing short of astounding. Some readers pen comprehensive plotlines with vivid character descriptions that breathe life into their envisioned worlds. Others choose a more abstract approach, crafting mere fragments of scenes or intriguing situations that capture their imagination.

Griff is humbled by the trust bestowed upon him by his readers. Their unwavering faith in his storytelling prowess is both a privilege and a responsibility he holds dear. Determined to honor their dedication and the exuberance they bring to his craft, he resolves to create an announcement that will further fuel their creativity.

Seated at his writing desk, Griff pens a carefully worded missive, inviting his audience to join him in weaving tales that push the boundaries of imagination. He encourages them to unleash their wildest notions, assuring them that no concept will be deemed too audacious. After all, his enduring mantra has always been, "No kink is too kinky."

Griff feels a flutter of excitement in his heart with the announcement destined to grace his website and adorn the pages of his upcoming books and stories. His readers are an integral part of his creative journey, and he knows that their collaboration will elevate his work to heights he can scarcely conceive. As the ink dries on his announcement, he sends it forth into the digital world, eagerly awaiting the responses that will soon fill his inbox. Griff yearns to unravel the enigma of their collective imaginations and the stories that will emerge from the amalgamation of their dreams and his craft.

In the following days, the flood of ideas surges again, and Griff finds himself immersed in a treasure trove of inspiration. Each email contains a universe of passion and desire, waiting to be crafted into compelling narratives that delight his readers.

With boundless enthusiasm, he delves into the task at hand, weaving together the threads of his readers' ideas with his inimitable style. The result is a collection of tales that span the spectrum of human desires, transporting readers to familiar and unexplored realms.

Griff and his readers form an unbreakable bond through their shared creativity, a communion of hearts and minds united by the power of storytelling. The journey ahead promises adventure, passion, and revelations, and together, they venture forth into the uncharted territories of the human imagination, leaving a trail of tantalizing tales in their wake.

To contribute story ideas, readers are invited to email Griff at: Griff.Holland.Writer@gmail.com

Printed in Great Britain
by Amazon

35284148R00076